Praise for The Illui

"Wohl is a force, taking th
Tolkien and running wit
Erica Summers, author o

"Fast-paced with action and mystery. You will be gripping the pages to find out what happens next. I need to second book now! This stands out. I'm already a big fan of this series and author!"
- Alexandria Williams, book reviewer

"I am ready for the next book! Please let there be one!" -Stephanie Mansour, Reviewer

"I was captivated from the start!" - Amazon reviewer

"I was waiting for it to let up and slow down but shockingly it didn't. The characters are well thought out and add so much to the story, driving it along getting you caught up in the moments. I recommend this book over and over." - Amazon reviewer

"From the very first page, this book sweeps you into another world and doesn't let you leave…" - Amazon reviewer

"The world is wonderfully crafted from the whiskey to the characters."- Amazon reviewer

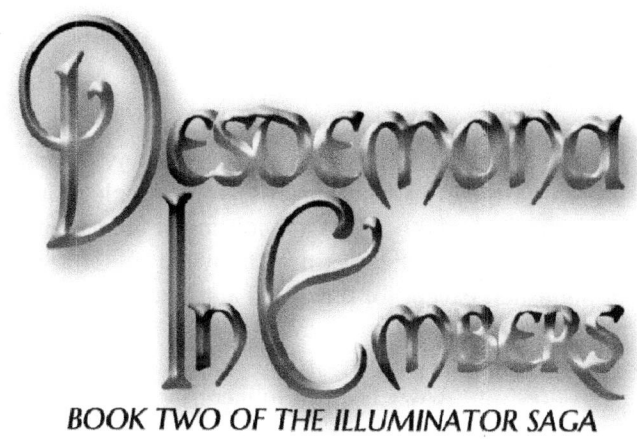

Desdemona In Embers

BOOK TWO OF THE ILLUMINATOR SAGA

BY

HEATHER WOHL

Desdemona in Embers: *Book Two of the Illuminator Saga*

Copyright © 2023 by Heather Wohl.

Casper, Wyoming, United States

All Rights Reserved.

No part of this book may be reproduced in any manner, or transmitted in any form or by any means, electronic, mechanical, photocopying, recording or otherwise, without express written permission by the author(s) and or publisher, except for the use of a brief quotation in a book review.

www.heatherwohl.com

www.rustyogrepublishing.com

This book is a work of fiction. Names, characters, places, events, organizations and incidents are either part of the author's imagination or are used fictitiously.
Any resemblance to actual persons, living or dead, or actual events is purely coincidental.

Cover Design by Erica Summers

This book is dedicated to the original badass, Quistix's inspiration, Erica Summers.

This is also dedicated to my fellow chronic pain and chronic illness fighters, when life gets tough, remember you are tougher.

And last but never least, I dedicate this to Rick Wohl, for loving me through it all.

DESDEMONA IN EMBERS

More by Heather Wohl

Books:

From Ashes: Book One of the Illuminator Saga
Desdemona in Embers: Book Two of the Illuminator Saga
Call of the Wyl (with Aurora Alba)
Writhe (with Erica Summers)

Published Short Stories:

"Prayers to Poseidon" - *An Ancient Curse* Vol 2
"Flesh Tag" - *Books of Horror Community* Vol.4

DESDEMONA IN EMBERS

Reviews

If you could take the time to leave an honest review after you've read this book, we would greatly appreciate it. We respect your time and promise it doesn't *have* to be long and eloquent. Even a few words will do!

As a small publishing house, every review helps others determine if this book is right for them and greatly increases our chances of being discovered by someone else who might enjoy it.

A Note From The Ogres

Even though this book was proofread thoroughly by editors, proofreaders, and ARC readers, mistakes happen. We want our readers to have the best experience possible. If you spot any spelling, grammatical, or formatting errors, please feel free to reach out to us at: Rustyogrepublishing@gmail.com

FROM ASHES: BOOK ONE OF THE ILLUMINATOR SAGA

RECAP

Quistix Daedumal, a half-elf blacksmith from the backwoods of Bellanue, lost her son and nearly everything she owned in a tragic fire set by a notorious bandit. Months later, the feral woman robbed an ewanian near her new home in the woods and discovered a wounded wyl, Twitch, in one of the crates. She aided in his recovery and he asked her out to dinner in Adum where he offered to help her find the Emerald Bandit she sought revenge from. With reluctance, she agreed and they traveled north to Silvercrest. They soon encountered an adorable dragonling, Frok, and her well-read esteg caretaker, Aurora, and after a battle with angered inelm tree-people, they decided to band together as a group.

Meanwhile, Destoria's queen, Exos Tempest, legalized a potent, addictive drug called dikeeka. Much to her displeasure, Vervaine (the queen's sister) and Arias (the head of the Obsidian guard) stoke the flames of their forbidden romance. Torn between micromanaging Vervaine's province and battling her mysterious illness, Exos struggled to maintain control of Destoria and its increasingly agitated people.

Born out of a desperate need, Exos employed the help of a shunned, experienced magic-wielding quichyrd, Ceosteol. Living up to her end of the bargain, Ceosteol assisted Exos in her dastardly deeds, but didn't receive the pardon she was promised.

After some adventure-filled missteps, Quistix and her new friends arrived at the Bandit's Den with a bloodlust for Soren, the bandit who killed her son, Danson, racing through her mind.

During the showdown in the Emerald Bandit's den, Quistix revealed previously undiscovered and powerful magical abilities.

Seeking answers, the group headed to Apex, the floating city containing the Institute of Magic. Exos, seeking the elusive Illuminator Ceosteol insisted would cure her disease, became more desperate to find Quistix, the alleged owner of the Illuminator, dead or alive.

Omen, a cursed human banished to a life of pain in eternal flame, has been told in no uncertain terms that he must bring back the Illuminator to Exos or die. Quistix is labeled a wanted woman by Queen Exos, inspiring unhelpful and vague wanted posters to be disseminated around the isle.

With all eyes searching for Quistix and her crew, they are forced into the shadows. But as the harsh and unforgiving weather of Evolt approaches, they must decide on a new course. As the band of outlawed outcasts come to rest for the evening, they are awoken by an unwanted guest bearing undead abominations.

Out of time, Exos needed to find Quistix and the Illuminator, or to die trying.

DESDEMONA IN EMBERS

[Map of the Isle of Destoria showing regions including Apex, Evolt, Silverc—, and Obsidia, with locations such as Crypt of Hadena, Glacier Straight, Silver Storm Tundra, Strogsend Brig, Apex City, The Evolt Snow Fields, Stoneward Prison, Enewain, Starlight Lake, Platinum Cape, Evolt City, Ryu Cove, Arrowside, Gorglide Rift, Fulgore Can—, Raven Cairn, Emerald River, The Lush Beaver, Taudale Farms, Crow Falls, Grustin Farm, Strogsend River, Tamber Falls, Glistening Brook, Emerald Bandit Den, Grim Harbor Farms, Dalo, Lair of the Twisted, Symph Grove, Oshedon, Brittle Moor, Kouver Farmstead, Southgulch Plantation, Ravenspell Bay, Soundless Shallows, Raging Infernal Caverns, Barerock, Bellaneau City, Bandit's Delta]

Scan here for an expanded full-color map of the Isle of Destoria

A complete creature glossary of all of the Isle of Destoria's beings is available in the back of this book.

1

*Wilds of Silvercrest,
Silvercrest*

As the moons loomed high overhead in their eternal game of chase, Quistix awoke to the sound of crunching leaves in the distance.

She picked up *Swordbreaker*, resting near the smoldering fire they'd encircled just a few hours prior when its blaze was mighty. Her heart pounded as the noise moved closer. She anxiously wound her fingers through the bloodied, tattered cloth tied around the ax handle, a keepsake from the night her son died. Her hands warmed the steel handle as her body temperature rose. Her eyes shifted from flecks of gold to the palest of yellows.

A pitch-black silhouette appeared behind a tree nearby, its blue eyes lighting up the tree trunk. The rot of meat and rancid bile was in the air.

It was a tailed infernal, a necromanced creature not found in her home province of Bellaneau. She'd never seen one in the wild. Worse, yet, there were *two*. The tailed infernals stepped out from behind a massive tree, tethered to a man with blue eyes by a two-chain leash.

Adrenaline pounded through Quistix's veins.

"*Sede.*" The intruder hissed, his voice like several individual voices morphed in unison. The decaying wolf-like heads of the infernals snarled, hungry for their next meal. Globs of drool dripped from their jowls and smoldered as they contacted the frozen grass below. A green hue glowed from beneath loose patches of skin. The shackles around their necks dug deep as they tugged closer.

"Who goes there?" It was more like an order than a question from Quistix's mouth.

The man removed his hood, exposing the ever-lit blue flames licking his middle-aged features. The leather armor rubbed together as he pulled the snarling monstrosities back towards himself. *It was Omen.* The cursed human smiled. "You've been a hard elf to hunt, Quistix. All of Destoria has been looking for you."

"How do you know my name? Who are you?"

"I know *much* about you, *Lux Alba*." His lips formed a chilling smile beneath the rippling warmth. He removed one glove, switching hands to do the same with the other.

Soon, the cooking chains in his bare hands glowed orange with the heat. He cracked them like a whip against the creatures' foul, exposed ribs. "I want *the Illuminator*."

She reared back her ax, answering his request with aggression. "I keep telling you idiots I don't know what that *is*!"

"Exos will want to hear that from the horse's mouth." Omen released the creatures from the chains and bolted toward the elf, knocking *Swordbreaker* from her hand with the *clink* of his chains against the rugged metal of her ax.

Before she could react, he grabbed her by the throat and pinned her against a tree. He wrapped the molten chains around her wrists, expecting to hear her scream.

To hear her flesh sizzle.

But she stood calm, unaffected by the temperature of the metal.

The two tailed infernals ran toward the wyl like zombified panthers, graceful and decaying. Twitch shot toward his satchel as quickly as his feet would carry him.

Bound by chains, Quistix clasped Omen's wrists with her soot-smeared fingers, unharmed by the searing heat from his skin. He looked at her filthy yet unscathed hand with total confusion. Goosebumps arose.

The sudden feel of skin upon his own felt so foreign to him after all these years. Due to the hellish curse cast upon him by Exos's father, he hadn't felt a woman's touch in decades. Not since the flames had ravaged that too-eager prostitute in Lagdaloon. He could still see the betrayed look in her eyes. He recalled the shame he felt for accidentally ending the poor girl. He couldn't even bring himself to show his flaming face at her grave site in that scourge-filled town in the years since.

Here, someone was finally unphased by his furnace-like touch. As the rage brewed within her, he felt her skin grow hotter than his own.

"What... *are* you?" His synchronized voices whispered like a small choir of demons, his navy eyes astonishingly wide in the dim forest. Without thinking, he loosened his grip in pure fascination.

Quistix's eyes had turned white beneath his amazed gaze. The tree bark behind her was now popping and crackling from her heat. She smiled and choked out the words, "Damned if *I* know."

She exploded at him, her magical force blasting him with a fireball originating near his stomach. An ungodly scream escaped his mouth. Instead of being blown away, he held tight to her throat with his constricting, burning fist.

The infernals galloped toward the others. Frok screamed, but Aurora knew what to do. The creatures before her appeared exactly as they had been in a crudely drawn textbook she'd studied long ago.

They were mere inches from her as she yelled out, "*Aspergetur ex-spiritu!*"

Instantly, the tailed infernals slammed their grotesque corpses into the ground with incredible force. Putrefied skin decomposed into a noxious puddle beneath them, leaving only two skeletal piles of liquid goop at Aurora's hooves.

There was no time for celebration, however. Soon after their destruction, the infernal's bones shifted and rearranged themselves back into a singular two-headed, four-legged being, attached at the hips with a bony snake-like tail. Aurora skittered in panic as the bleach-white bony jaws snapped wild. Their eye sockets filled with electric green light.

With shaking hands, Twitch readied a jagged stone-tipped arrow and aimed at the heart of the foul beast.

"*Aeratgu!*" Omen screamed, and the beast regarded the magical term as a *stay* command, drool dripping from their eager fangs as they held in place. He needed her alive, which would be impossible if the infernals mangled the elf into minced meat.

Quistix struck Omen's forehead with a balled fist and sent the cursed human stumbling backward. Shaking off the searing pain in her hand, Quistix delivered a jump-kick to the center of Omen's chest with her leather boot. Omen flew backward, striking his pierced, flaming cranium against another tree. His vision blurred, and he laughed out in frustration as vibrant blue blood dribbled over his pearly teeth.

"Who sent you?!" She barked angrily.

The infernals' ears twitched unnaturally, and their heads snapped toward Quistix. She tugged *Swordbreaker* from the ground and readied it. The infernals lowered their heads, ready to pounce.

Aurora stood still, frozen in place by fear, unable to move. Frok whimpered from inside her hammock, shielding her eyes from what was sure to be a gruesome end.

"Impetum!" Omen shouted. The infernals lunged toward Quistix.

Twitch snatched his bow and quiver from the log he had been sleeping beside just moments before. He turned to Aurora.

"Run!"

Aurora did as she was told, darting away on skittering hooves before returning for a final look. She watched as Twitch knocked an arrow and tilted his head, signaling for her to leave. She nodded and darted into the inky darkness beyond.

Quistix swung her ax at the first of the infernals, lopping off one of the heads of the two-headed beast.

An arrow went through the back of the head of the second snapping maw. Its coiled tail lunged for her, narrowly missing and striking the tree behind her as she rolled out of the way.

The second infernal lunged on top of her, pinning her to the ground. Both sets of rotting, hole-filled jowls dribbled acidic drool onto her cheeks.

A second arrow shot through both heads, just inches above Quistix's nose. The stitched figure collapsed on top of her as its snake tail reared up and struck the ground beside her face. Quistix struggled to shove the hefty infernal from her chest. Twitch fired another arrow, missing the small, striking target.

Quistix screamed as she hurled the heavy figure over her head, tossing it onto its back and pinning its venomous snake tail to the ground. Omen stepped behind her and held his emerald-encrusted dagger to her throat.

"Enough! It's high time you meet our Queen." Omen heard the creaking as Twitch tugged the string of his bow, arrow knocked, arrowhead trained on their unwelcome intruder.

"Let her go," Twitch ordered, his voice so stern he even surprised himself a little.

Omen chuckled, jerking Quistix this way and that, shoving his face from one side of her head to the other like a deadly game of peek-a-boo.

"You wouldn't risk her life to take mine, now, would you? Go ahead. *Shoot*."

Twitch slowly lowered his bow. Quistix groaned in defeat.

"Good choice." Omen's voices almost hissed with satisfaction. "Now, give me the damn Illuminator!"

"How many times do I have to say it before it gets through your thick skull? We. Don't. Know. What. That. Is. Got it?!" Quistix snarled.

Omen looked back at her, stunned. "You're serious."

Twitch shrugged his shoulders. "Whatever it is, you and your boss wouldn't be burning cities and killing children if you weren't desperate. What do you want it for?"

Omen choked up his grip on the dagger, tugging the blade into the surface of Quistix's skin. "I'm the one asking the questions!"

Frok emerged from behind Omen, fluttering silently between his legs with thin vines dangling from her like an oversized sash.

Twitch glanced down at the movement, spotted Frok, and immediately returned his gaze to Omen.

"Alright," Twitch began, trying to keep him distracted. "I'm sorry, you are right. It's your show. Just don't hurt her."

"The Illuminator was crafted by Master Daedumal. It's written in his tomes. Master Tempest and her father discovered the secret to immortality. They worked together, using her father's knowledge and Master Daedumal's proclivity for black magic. Before the final solution was revealed, her traitorous father took their work and hid it somewhere. He couldn't take it back to Apex, where it could be found. It was, after all, against their idiotic rules regarding dark magic. So, where would he hide it? Who does he have left that he could leave it to? You!"

Quistix's eyes flashed white. Fury exploded like a flash of fire inside of her. Omen grew uncomfortable as her body's emanating heat surpassed his own.

"I haven't heard a word from that bastard in decades! He dropped me on my grandfather's doorstep and never came back. I wouldn't risk my life for a man who couldn't give a shit if I live or die."

Omen turned his gaze toward Quistix in surprise. His expression turned disheartened. "We'll let Exos be the judge of that."

Twitch quickly glanced down and saw Frok quietly tug a knot into place around Omen's ankles.

Quistix gripped Omen's hand and jerked the blade away from her throat, elbowing him in the ribs with her other arm. He grunted as she broke free of his grasp.

She leapt away. Twitch readied his bow as Omen stepped toward her, tripping over the tied vines and face-planting into the frosted leaves below.

Quistix kicked him onto his back and climbed on top of him, pinning his arms beneath her legs. She pressed his shoulders into the ground. "You're getting me a meeting with Queen Exos. We're gonna end this!"

Omen laughed, his multi-tonal voice echoing through the dense woods surrounding them. "No matter where you hide, she will find you. She'll burn Destoria down like her father if she must."

Twitch readied an arrow, aiming for Omen's flaming face. When his burning eyes noticed, he smiled brightly and vanished. As Twitch fired the arrow, the cursed human's body dissipated into a wisp of ethereal lapis smoke that drifted with the gentle night breeze into the midnight sky.

The arrow vibrated, buried in the dirt beside Quistix. The faint sound of Omen's multi-tonal laugh cackled darkly in the distance.

The multi-headed beast growled, tugging at its dead comrade, digging its gnarled claws into the dirt. It madly tore at them, fighting to close the gap between them, its matted hackles raised.

Paws trembling with fear, Twitch launched an arrow through one of the heads of the infernals. Even scared, his aim amazed Quistix.

Its slack jaw hung loose and lifeless from its conjoined body. Two legs of the creature collapsed. The animal tried to right itself as it toppled over on its side, flailing its other extremities. Twitch launched another, piercing the second skull.

The demonic entity finally dropped, unmoving on the ground. The snake-like tail coiled, baring its protruding fangs. With her emerald dagger, Quistix bent down, removed the reptilian head, and threw it hard into the black woods like a pitched ball.

She looked at the infernal, twin arrows stuck in its head like giant toothpicks through hideous *hors d'oeuvres*, then back at the wyl.

"Well, that… was impressive."

2

*The Amethyst Caverns,
The Obsidian Palace,
Obsidia*

Exos strummed her pale fingers along the edge of the wooden table, gazing at Omen. He adjusted in his seat uncomfortably, squeaking his noubald pants against the tiaga wood chair.

"Repeat it again. Make me understand." Exos leaned in.

He sighed, rubbing his flaming hands together beneath the table. "We have not received the biago berries yet. Otis read them the letter. Payment was given to the wyl. No one has seen him since."

"What letter?"

Omen produced the letter Durwin had given him. Exos read and crumpled it.

"Your men thought I wrote this?" She glanced at the floating torches of the amethyst cavern. "This is why wyls shouldn't be anywhere *near* money. So now this little shit has the coin *and* our product?" Exos felt the nearly uncontrollable urge to cough. She took a ragged breath and cleared her throat. "I'd order you to kill him, but you can't even do that with the copper-headed bitch." She growled and slammed her frail fist onto the table. "You keep failing me and failing me and failing me, Omen! How many chances must I give you?!"

Omen remained silent, his blazing blue gaze never leaving hers.

"You've made me look like a fool. Repeatedly!" She placed her hands flat on the table and thought for a moment, her tone calmer. "I'm disbanding the Emerald Bandits. You are no longer fit to lead anyone. I'll assemble another troupe for Biagio berry transport. From this day forward, if the bandits are found wearing the uniform or displaying emerald daggers in public, they'll be taken to the stocks for at least one year sentence. If I find out even *one of them* brings my name into talks of past illegal trade, I'll have Ceosteol afflict them with the same eternal curse she put upon you. Is that clear?"

Omen wouldn't wish his curse upon his worst enemy, much less comrades he'd come to care for. *Comrades he failed.* "Yes, Your Majesty."

"You're demoted. Your new command will be overseeing the Infernal Caverns. Enjoy your days as a jailer." She smirked cruelly and shooed him. "Get out of my sight."

3

*Wilds of Evolt,
Evolt*

Frok slept soundly inside her twisted hammock, undisturbed by the freezing winds and snowfall. Below, Aurora's pristine white coat fluffed itself in an attempt to combat the inhospitable temperatures of nightfall. Beside her, Twitch was wrapped in a too-long raakaby coat, leaving drag marks behind him in the snow.

A bloodied, limp tefly came into view in the moonlight. Its lifeless, horse-like head bobbed in and out of the snow unnaturally. Something was dragging its long, snarled mane through the pink, frozen flakes. Its chest and stomach bulged unevenly, like an embryonic mass kicking its mother's womb.

All at once, the movement stopped.

The bulge in the regal tefly's abdomen moved downward and pushed up a tunneled line of snow in front of the creature's hooves. A small head erupted from the snow and glared back at them. Everyone stood stone-still, gazing at the tiny foreign entity's icy blue eyes. Its pointed ears wriggled, tossing snow from their tips. Large fangs stuck out from its top jaw over its reddened lower lip.

The group remained stone-still.

The tefly corpse shifted again. Something small rapped on the ribs of the deer, knocking as if it were a door. Then, the animal's barrel chest collapsed all at once in the snow. Like kernels, six sickly, crimson heads popped out of the drift in front of the carrion, covered in flurries and ichor.

All bloodied and identical.

"They're tundra goblins," whispered Aurora. "They are simple. They only seek food and warmth. They won't hurt you as long as you don't hurt them." The goblins tilted their heads to Aurora as she approached.

As a hushed conversation began between the esteg and goblins, Quistix lowered her ax. The first to emerge shoved its paw towards Aurora's face. Aurora shook her head and nodded back to the group.

Suddenly, the goblins revealed sharpened six-inch claws all at once, long enough to turn Frok into sliced tuna steak in one motion.

Aurora walked backward toward the group, dumbstruck. "We had a good chat. They are, in fact, cold and hungry. The bad news is that they said they are going to eat us and use our bodies as shelter."

"What are they waiting for? Why haven't they attacked?" Twitch's brows knitted together in confusion.

"They are awaiting our response: *Surrender* or *war*," Aurora explained, shifting her feet uneasily. "Surrender means we will not protest as they eat us."

The goblins shouted, baring menacing teeth. "*Aje! Aje! Psime da tica!*"

Around them, snow banks rose and fell, undulating like white waves as a throng of goblins made their way beneath the snow toward them. Soon, nearly three dozen of the small creatures rushed out like a tiny army, hungry for blood.

A field of eyes, variants along the blue spectrum, squinted against howling blizzard winds. All chanting, "*Aje, aje, aje!*"

"Not today!" Quistix turned away from them and darted past a leafless tree. The others followed, racing uphill.

The little monsters gave chase up the mound. Quistix ran faster, the grade burning her thighs with every gallop. Whipping snow stung their eyes. Twitch struggled to keep up. Aurora galloped gracefully, snow swallowing her knobby angles.

As Quistix turned her head back to the direction she was running, she realized she was about to careen off of a steep, icy cliff. Falling off it would mean certain death, judging by the depths. She screamed and stopped in the nick of time, her boots sliding on the icy rock face near the edge. The swarm of critters growled and hissed behind them.

"This was not in any of the books. None of the battle tactics, evasive maneuvers, and peace-keeping arguments I've read about seem to be applicable." Aurora watched as the snarling goblins spoke amongst themselves, eyes trained on the motley bunch of intruders.

Frok mustered her courage and fluttered from her cocoon, giving her fiercest look to the goblins. "Nobody's gonna hurt my fwends!" Frok erupted in a tiny battle cry, swiping at the air. The pleom shot like a rocket at the first goblin and smacked it hard in the nose with her clawed hand.

Its eyes watered from the impact. It bared its teeth and growled, "*biw.*"

With that simple utterance, the miniature army of violent creatures attacked. Quistix swiped at several with her ax. They evaded. One latched onto her knuckles, bit down hard, and forced her to drop *Swordbreaker*.

Her eyes grew white with fury.

Another leaped onto Quistix, sinking its brutal saw-like teeth into the flesh of her palm. She pried its jaws from her hand and hurled the creature over the cliff, turning back to the tiny army.

Thick drifts of snow moved like foamy, white ocean waves as more rumbled beneath, coming to the aid of the first wave of goblins.

Twitch aimed at a line of three with his bow, waiting for the moment when they might align. Arrowheads were scarce in this snowy tundra. He had to be precise.

The goblins charged at them, uttering tiny cries of war in another tongue. Aurora used her rack to smack several goblins, one at a time, over the cliff's edge before finally being overrun and pinned to the ground. Several goblins climbed atop the esteg, chewing her ankles and iridescent antlers. She bleated in pain. "*Ba-aa-aa-aa!*"

Twitch fired his arrow, spearing all three of the minuscule hellions with one shot.

Frok flew to Aurora's aid but was snatched by a clawed hand out of mid-air. Frok squealed as one started to gnash at her scaly foot with its sharpened fangs.

Quistix roundhouse kicked three of them into their comrades and ran to Frok and Aurora's side, slicing goblins with her emerald dagger. Three tundra goblins carried *Swordbreaker*, leaning it into the air and dropping it like a guillotine near Aurora's throat. As the ax plunked into the snow, the critters struggled to lift it. Quistix kicked them high into the sky, connecting hard with her noubald boots.

A stray goblin leaped onto her boot and gnawed through with serrated teeth, and another latched into the skin of her calf. Adrenaline punched through her veins as she reached for Frok, whose head was inches from the mouth of a starving goblin. She screamed.

The snow melted in a circle around her. She looked down. The veins inside of her arm glowed electric blue.

It was happening again.

The elf radiated intense heat that grew with her anger. The snow around her melted off the craggy rocks, dribbling like a stream down the course terrain. The tundra goblins had frozen in shock at the sight of it.

From her palms, a fireball materialized. It shot fast, striking a hoard of hairy winter creatures and erupting a dormant, flaking tiaga tree beyond them into a scorching torch of roaring fire. A pile of singed bodies rolled in the melting snow, trying to snuff the fiery blaze to cool their blistering skin. As the fight slowed, Quistix's eyes returned to their normal shade, and Aurora's horns lit up a brighter day glo green, reflecting color off the watery snow pile beside her as she healed the bite and claw marks that ravaged her esteg body with the caress of her velvety antlers.

Quistix quickly carried Frok's broken little body over to Aurora. The glowing green light engulfed the weakened dragonling, and her bloodied slash marks and torn wing healed at a fascinating rate.

Once mended, Twitch took the pleom gently in his paws, clutching her trembling little body tightly. "I thought you were a goner! Don't you ever die on me!" Twitch nuzzled her with his wet nose. She wrapped her little pink claws around his snout and hugged it lovingly.

A single goblin stepped in front of the others and shouted, "*Atig sone!*"

Those around it joined in on its chant, lifting their furry paws in the air. The chant spread to the rest of the goblins. Within moments, they all began a deafening chant, yelling out excitedly, "*Atig sone!*"

Quistix stood dumbfounded. None attacked. Instead, three of them offered up *Swordbreaker*, barely able to handle its hefty weight between them. She took the weapon, now covered in blood and goblin drool.

"*Atig sone! Atig sone!*" They shouted in unison, bowing reverently and kneeling before her.

"*Atig!*" The little one pointed to the fire growing in the treetops. "*Sone!*" A now-docile goblin pointed with its tiny, furry hand to Quistix and forced a too-wide smile across its demonic-looking face. She looked at the esteg, completely confused.

Aurora gave a weak grin and yelled out, "*Atig sone...* it means *goddess of fire.*"

4

Wilds of Evolt,
Evolt

The large group of goblins devoured their dead for sustenance. Twitch was nestled between two creatures gnawing on jostling bones, licking each clean, grinding off the cartilage. Nothing went to waste.

The tree blazed in the middle of them all, its heat dwindling.

Having already voraciously eaten her portion of smoked goblin meat, Quistix walked to the edge of the cliff where she had nearly fallen to her death a mere hour before. She looked out into the starry night sky, savoring the expansive view. Two moons of orange and one of solemn blue drifted in the night sky in near-perfect alignment. She closed her gold-flecked eyes and pictured fire erupting from her palms.

After several seconds, Quistix looked at her splayed hand.

Nothing.

She thought about what Danson's reaction would have been if he'd seen her perform these strange feats. She imagined he would look at her, those giant eyes so full of awe and wonder. He already viewed her as his hero, his protector. Even though she'd failed him miserably the day, Soren showed his face and snatched the rest of his life from him.

From them both.

And Roland? *Would he look at me like a Goddess,* she wondered, not with eyes filled with temperate years-long love but with passion for her otherworldly skills. As anguish rippled over her like ebbing waves, dragging her down below the sadness, she looked to her feet...

The snow had melted in a ten-foot diameter around her, and where it had been, the world beneath sprouted anew. Dead spots of iced-over yellow grass melted from the freeze and filled in with new luscious patches of shamrocks and clovers. Timid tulips and rambunctious roses sprung up from leaf detritus, rooted steadfastly in the softened soil. The donik trees near her budded with new growth, unfurling baby leaves in unison. The rest of the tundra was void of life – save for the gnawing goblins feasting loudly and her travel companions – but in the area around her, the blossoming earth was alive, blooming like springtime.

The nearby crunch of hooves in the snow tore Quistix from her frustrated thoughts.

"Are you alright?" Aurora sounded concerned, eyes drifting from the rich foliage beneath her hooves to the deep, glimmering holler of pristine snow that sprawled endlessly below.

"Yes, just... trying to understand. Or... *practice*." Her words sounded more like a confused question than a response.

Aurora held her head up, regal in the dueling colors of the moons. "You have the gift. When we get to Apex, do not be put off if you encounter people who are displeased with your powers. Many envy those with natural abilities who have not honed their skills. It's seen as a waste, a rejection of your magical heritage."

"I didn't even know I had... *this*... until a few days ago." She held up her grimy hands, roughened from the harsh elements and her decades-long occupation.

"Not everyone will care. Those born with abilities are capable of stronger magic than those who train."

The sound of bone snapping made Aurora turn, hooves skittering in fear. She sighed upon the realization that it was from two goblins fighting over their dead kin's ribcage. Their gazes again turned outward toward the gorgeous frozen landscape.

"I didn't know my parents, but I don't think my grandfather practiced magic. He was a blacksmith."

"It doesn't mean he wasn't magical. It's in you. You're a natural." Aurora motioned to a patch of moonlit greenery at her feet. Newly budded fauna swayed gently in the frosty winds. Aurora ripped a chunk of clover up with her mouth and chewed.

"You know, my grandfather taught me how to make potions as a kid." Quistix smiled a little. "He was stern, to say the least. But he soon saw I had a knack for finding ingredients. And I could smell when they'd mixed correctly. He said I was a natural too."

Aurora swallowed her mouthful of grass, enjoying every savory blade. "You practiced. Gained skill. You were in an environment that nurtured your natural abilities." She chewed another mouthful of grass and swallowed. "There are drawbacks to natural versus learned magic."

"How so?" Quistix's voice wavered.

"Natural-born magical entities are never able to *fully* control their skills. Ruled by emotion and mental manipulation, there remains an element of surprise to your magic. For example, you may someday wish to cast a fireball at your enemy but, under the wrong circumstances, could accidentally freeze your comrade solid instead. After watching you, I can say that when you're angered, you lean towards *Ave Ignis*, loosely translating to *fire magic*." She nodded her head at the burning remnants of the tree behind them that Quistix had set on fire hours earlier.

"*Ave Ignis.* Hmm." Quistix whispered the words, thick with her billowing breath, into the arctic air.

"When melancholy, you favor environmental magics or *Aliquam Venenatis.* That's grass, water, ice, rainstorms, and so on." Aurora nodded down at the vibrant patch of vegetation below Quistix's boots.

She stared at the esteg, for the first time, truly in awe of the knowledge she possessed.

"Lastly, *fear*. Fear makes people unpredictable, and results are randomized. The struggle, for your kind, is the control of that emotion. You're magically at your most *dangerous* when you are afraid."

"Oh, that's great." Quistix couldn't help but let the sarcasm ooze from her voice through the frozen air. "Guess I'll just stop being afraid. Problem solved."

5

*Ceosteol's Underground Lair,
Desdemona Undergrounds,
Willowdale*

A child's cold body lay on the bedding of sticks and leaves inside Ceosteol's hovel. Scuttling around with muddied talons, she fumbled through the jars along shelves carved into the dirt beside her rusty pot. The spoon stirred on its own, swirling, bubbling, dark liquid. She gasped in excitement as she pulled free a glass container. A single leech sluggishly inched along the bottom.

"Last one's lucky," she said aloud. She uncorked the jar and shook it furiously until the leech slapped onto her hand. Shivers of excitement traveled up the feathers on her back beneath her cloak. She danced over to the rusty, floating pot and dumped it in.

"Last bit, just a drop," she said aloud to no one.

Today, her family would grow by one more. Shivering with anticipation, she rolled the sleeve of her robe, exposing the skinny bird-like arm beneath. Along other inch-long, parallel scars, she dragged her razored talon along the flesh to make a fresh slice. Thick as molasses, electric green liquid seethed from the seam in her scaly flesh. She scooped the syrupy liquid in her claw and flung it into the pot. The bubbling blackness turned gangrene. She pulled the spoon out of the pot. The leech latched on. Cautiously, she plucked it off. Emerald-stained teeth chittered and snapped from its underbelly.

"Perfection, as always." She chuckled to herself.

She swooped toward the young human. The little girl had dirt and autumn leaves tangled in her snarled hair. Her blue eyes were open, fogged with the haze of death. Her porcelain skin was marred by pox and scratches, telltale signs of an infestation that claimed many other poor, emaciated children like her who spent a good deal of time in the wild.

Ceosteol lifted the little girl's head and dug a talon into the flesh at the base of her skull. She reached beneath with her other hand and forced the leech inside of the opening. It hungrily slithered inside.

"They buried you like trash. They don't see you like I do." Ceosteol cooed. She recalled the name on the grave she'd exhumed only hours before.

"Rosey, you are welcome here. You will never be thrown away again."

While her slithering servant gnashed its way into position, Ceosteol peered down at the girl, a smile forming at the corners of her beak. She was perfect.

Her pupils expanded, swallowing up the sclera and iris, spreading like an ink drop through the whites of her eyes until the whole orb was solid black.

The child blinked.

Ceosteol clapped her claws joyfully. "Welcome, my darling!"

The child stared ahead, wide-eyed with confusion. Her arms jerked and popped as she tried to prop herself up on both elbows. Rosey sat up, each vertebrae giving a stiff snap as she twisted at the waist and swung her feet onto the dirt floor. She stood before Ceosteol for a long moment, trying to understand.

"Would you like to meet the rest of the family?"

The girl nodded, but her head tumbled forward limply on her neck. Ceosteol pulled her head back by the hair and pressed down, the sound of broken bones grinding against each other echoing off the walls. The quichyrd gave her an encouraging pat on the back and guided her toward the muddy steps of the hovel.

"Revelare," Ceosteol growled.

The boulder blocking the entrance rolled to one side, uncovering the exit. As they walked up the stairs, dozens of children came into view, standing eerily in the golden glow of dawn. Deep in the woods, the veil of fog was lifting. Streams of light tickled their pale faces from between a forest speckled with bare donik trees.

The children twisted their heads and bodies toward the new arrival in unison. Their black eyes, hollow and lifeless, stared blankly. Their expressions remained cold. Unphased.

"Say hello to your new sister," Ceosteol said, more of an order than a request.

The children spoke flatly, all at once:

"*Hello, Rosey.*"

She peered up at Ceosteol, who smiled from the edges of her beak. "Welcome home, darling."

6

*Harpy Stables, Ruby Palace,
Desdemona,
Willowdale*

Several farmhands cautiously held hunks of meat toward massive creatures, jerking their hands away once the quick snapping beaks lunged at it. They were feeding the vibrant-feathered harpies noubald steaks by the bucketful.

Arias paid no notice. He tugged the reins and goaded his harpy forward, guiding it down from the air into an unoccupied stall. It landed with a soft thud in the bed of hay piled within the walls. He hurriedly tied the reins and stormed through the field, locking his eyes on the castle. Suddenly, he spotted Exos and a gaggle of her guards and quickly changed course.

It was exactly who he'd come to see.

"Where is she?! Where did you take Vervaine?!" Arias snapped, taking long, aggressive steps to close the gap between them. Several guards intercepted defensively.

Exos stood wide-eyed in shock. "Arias! What a pleasant surprise! Gentlemen, a moment of privacy." Exos gestured her men away. After a brief hesitation, the guards stepped toward the gates and motioned for the farmhands to leave. They obliged.

As soon as the doors shut, Exos returned her attention to the wild-eyed man in front of her. "Vervaine is where she should be: learning a valuable lesson in *loyalty*."

"Do you think this is a *game*?" Arias stepped toward her. His height and muscular build, while formidable, did not intimidate Exos in the slightest.

"You and Vervaine were never meant to be. She was a *dalliance*. A meek little red flag you waved to get my attention. It worked. You *have* my attention."

"You're *sick*. Your ego is like nothing I've ever seen before. Being with her wasn't a way to get to *you*. Your *majesty*," He ground his teeth, "not everything is about *you*. Jealousy! *That's* what this *is*." Arias turned his back, frustrated.

Exos unbuttoned her white fur shawl, exposing alabaster cleavage hoisted high above a red lace neckline. "Join me here in Desdemona. I'll demote Ives and promote you to head of the guard. We will bring honor to your kind. Show the people how civilized and brave akaih can be. Don't be selfish. This is a golden opportunity for you and your *people*. Come, be by my side. Show Destoria what you're made of. Lead an army. Lead *the* army!"

Arias turned toward her, his brows scrunched in confusion, stomach churning with mixed emotions. Exos stepped to him and stared seductively, his hardened gaze unwilling to meet hers. His stomach flipped at her flippant reaction to such a cold, familial betrayal.

"Every bit of me misses every bit of you." She added, swirling a finger along his chest plate.

The image of Vervaine lying in bed beside him forced its way to the forefront of his mind. He chastised himself for his body's reflexive reaction to being caressed by a beautiful woman.

As her touch moved lower to his groin, he grumbled, the only response he could muster. "Are you finished?"

Exos recoiled. "Pride and stubbornness. It's precisely what infuriates *and* attracts me about you."

Arias walked back toward his harpy's stable and grabbed the reins. "I'm going to find her one way or another."

"Enough! This is no longer a negotiation. It's a royal *order*. If you disregard your new command as head of the Destorian army, I'll consider it a direct violation and have you arrested for treason so you can enjoy a similar fate to your little damsel whore." She stared daggers at him. "So what will it be? One of the highest positions in the land and the restoration of faith in your kind? Or rotting in a cell somewhere far away until those horns of yours turn to dust?"

Arias clenched his fists around the harpy's reigns. "You aren't leaving me any choice, are you then?" He bit the inside of his cheek in anger until it bled. "I suppose you win. Once again."

The weight of the words nearly crushed him.

"No, Arias, defeat is declared once a battle *ends*. This is far from over." She answered smugly. "Guard!" The beckoned man jogged through the door with something clutched in his hand. Exos smiled. "Gather what's left of the council and *Ives the Unbreakable* and summon them all to the meeting room. There's to be an announcement! Arias here is going to be formally inaugurated as the new head of the royal guard."

Arias tensed his jaw. Balling his fist, he swung at the wall beside him, shattering the wooden boards, growling in defeat.

"Very well, Your Majesty." He bowed, ignoring the enraged akaih behind him, and handed her a piece of parchment with a seal. "This just arrived. A symph delivered it but a moment ago. It appears to be *Omen's* seal, your majesty."

She unfurled the paper and read it. Her joy dissipated almost immediately, leaving behind a worried frown on her face. She crumpled the paper in her palm, digging her nails into her own flesh until she drew blood.

7

*The Raging Infernal Caverns,
Southern Obsidia*

An iguana skittered along the red, dusty rocks in a blur, weaving, and diving through the jagged terrain in search of a place to hide. With no clue where it had just been thrown, it scanned quickly for cover.

"Feeding time, boys." Omen's voice growled. The sound of bars closing echoed through the dark, dry chamber. The place was a charred desert hellscape with bars. The light was scarce. Food was scarcer.

A scarlet symph circled overhead, emaciated, eager to attack some prey before it perished. It zeroed in, trying to anticipate the reptile's movements. The lizard darted into a crevice and skittered onward, deep into darkness. After several moments of stillness, the animal's heartbeat slowed.

A popping noise sounded behind it, and the iguana scrambled to turn. A pair of foggy crimson eyes stared from centimeters away beneath a leather hood shrouded by darkness.

Except for the eyes. *Those dead, unblinking, foggy red eyes…*

The reaper focused its fiendish gaze on the petrified animal and clasped the iguana in its cold, dead hand. Invigorated by its terror, it absorbed the emotions of the feeble creature in its grasp. The iguana's restorative fear surged through its fingers. It savored the sweet, stolen emotion as if it were a delicacy.

Exos strode down the cavern's hall, hugging her full-length snow fox fur coat against the tightly-cinched, ornate corset beneath. She clicked her polished black fingernails along the iron bars of her sister's holding cell. The scent of dried blood wafted into her nostrils.

Vervaine lay on the craggy stone floor, curled into a ball in a tattered prisoner gown, which was now torn and bloodied. The bruises on her back, legs, and arms were visible even in the dim torchlight. A dead-eyed crimson soul reaper floated ominously behind, its signature red hood pulled low, shadowing its dead human face. They were Exos' creation, feeding on the fear and torture of the living.

"Mmmm, the soul reapers are creatures after my own heart. The pleasure of watching things squirm beneath your gaze is," Exos inhaled the noxious scent of the cavern with a smile, "*intoxicating.*"

Vervaine struggled to stand, legs quaking beneath her. She used all of her remaining energy to keep herself from swaying. As she shuffled toward the bars, Exos could see her eyes were both blackened. Blood dribbled from a cut in her lip and a slice in her eyebrow. Her neck was purpled by thin handprints.

Vervaine walked to the edge of her cage. She could feel the magic coursing through the bars, fortifying them, halting her own use of magic. It was a trick that had Ceosteol's name written all over it. In her mind, she cursed the clever quichyrd every day.

"Would you like to know what you must do to get out of this hell hole?" Exos asked smugly, reveling in the power she held in this moment.

"No." Vervaine's response was simple, yet she took every bit of wind from her sister's sails.

"No?"

"No. Father twisted you into his own little dutiful demon. Cold. Unpredictable. Unfeeling. At least when I'm here, I know what I can expect from these creatures. They have simple intentions. Simple rules, needs, and desires. *You*, on the other hand," Vervaine made the *pfft* noise with her sliced mouth and leaned in close. "You know you can't kill me. You *need* me. I sweep up the destruction in your wake and reassemble it into something beautiful. We both know I am why you are seen as successful and not the absolute tumultuous, temperamental force of utter chaos you are."

Exos could feel her cheeks growing hot with rage.

"As soon as I am out of here, everyone will know what you've done. The bloodied rags. The coughing fits. I've known you were sick and said nothing. I didn't want the crown. I have never been a threat to you. But now," She laughed heartily, "*everyone will know*." Vervaine swept a filthy lock of hair behind her pointed ear and grinned with satisfaction. Then she sucked her bloodied lip and spat, staining the white fur of Exos' coat with bloodied saliva.

"You... *ungrateful* piece–" Exos coughed hard, and she clasped her hand quickly over her mouth. She felt an alarming amount of her own fresh blood spatter on her palms.

"Oooh, that's a bad cough. Sounds *deadly*." Vervaine clasped the bars and stuck her head through as far as she could. "Well, one can only *hope*."

8

*Outside City Limits,
Raven Cairn, Evolt*

An icy squall raged through Evolt. The entrance of Raven Cairn bustled with exhausted workers in coyote-fur coats. Quistix dug her scuffed leather boots up what remained of the crunchy, flake-dusted path and looked around. Up ahead, in front of the high stone walls around the city, a portly barbarian commander on a white donik wood sleigh mushed a pack of straining gray mutts, oblivious to their crew in the tree line. Aurora's eyes glowered with disgust, her gaze locked on his fur coat.

Beyond the city walls, a massive iron statue of a giant, his weapon thrust into the base, stood erect in the town center.

"Whoa!" Frok cooed, buzzing around the base of the sculpture to take it all in. "Who is dat?"

"That's *Standorr*, the founder of Evolt. It's rumored this town was built by the giant. One text I came across even said the locals believe that giants, in a fit of anger, smashed their fists down into the icy tundra and blasted dirt bowls right out of the isle, which is why all of the cities in Evolt are built in cratered pits." Aurora spouted off. "Standorr is just one of many giants that Evoltians look up to."

There was a moment of silence between them as they drank in their chilled surroundings, their noses and cheeks red and raw from the freezing winds.

Quistix turned to Aurora, and, with sadness in her voice, she spoke. "I think it's time for you to head to the cave. Can't risk any of these trappers and whatnot seeing you. We are going to go get a good night's rest and a hot meal. Tomorrow's going to be a big day. I promise, when we meet in the morning, I'll bring hot food and fresh water for you."

Aurora nodded solemnly. She felt like an outcast, often unable to do things with her traveling companions.

"I'm sorry, Aurora. I really am. I wish you could go with us. We just can't risk anything happening to you."

"I understand. I'd rather not become another rack on the wall either." She lifted her head, her green antlers pulsing. "Frok, stay with Twitch. I'll see you in the morning."

The pleom's watering eyes were devastated. "Otay, 'Rora."

"Eat some cheese for me." Aurora managed a melancholy smile.

"No!" Quistix laughed. "No cheese. You'll gas us right out of our room. If you eat cheese, you're sleeping on the roof!"

Aurora chuckled and trotted off, bee-lining for the cave they'd cleared an hour or so before reaching Raven Cairn.

Quistix marched onward, and Twitch followed, the pudgy pink pleom nestled deep in the crook of the wyl's furry arm. They approached the base of the statue. Smooth curves and chiseled angles portrayed a lifelike giant in a lush pelt overcoat, slamming his mammoth sword into the ground. The elf couldn't help but feel awe befall her as she soaked in the painstaking detail and metal craftsmanship, unlike anything she'd ever seen back in Bellaneau.

Behind the statue, Quistix spotted a building, clearly labeled even through the white haze of the falling snow. *The Broken Wing Tavern & Inn*.

***

The interior was so raucous that Quistix could barely hear herself think. The main hall seemed much larger once inside. Lute music oozed from the back, only audible during lulls in patrons' conversations. A cluster of winter-clad men gathered at the back, each leaving the bar with a freshly filled beverage in hand.

Quistix shoved through wads of patrons without apology and wedged herself between two people at the bartop, waving to the bartender for a drink. He glanced her way, distracted almost instantly by a snapping pair of fingers in front of Quistix's face. There were far too many people in her personal space. Next to her, a partially obscured human face sneered from beneath the hood of a gray coyote fur coat. All pockmarked skin and rotted teeth. He grabbed her arm and tried to tug her away from the bar.

She *immediately* punched him in the throat.

His gasps and raspy breathing eased. She turned back to the bar. Nearly a dozen sets of terrified eyes locked on her. She nodded to a couple on stools nearby, and they rose and left. Whispers filled the air. She tapped on the stone bar slab and managed a half-grin up at the charming semdrog behind the bar. Her icy hands pressed against the smooth granite. She could feel the intense cold seeping up into her palms.

The studly, blue creature smiled. He had a slick, lizard-like texture to his glacier-blue skin that blended flawlessly up into a stark-white face. His sideways-blinking eyes startled her.

"Welcome to Raven Cairn." The semdrog held out his hand, and she took it. An almost painful bolt of cold rushed through her palm like an icy burst of lightning. She immediately pulled back, her eyes open wide. He didn't seem to mind. His light giggle told her that it happened frequently and that the shock was intentional. "Name's Oravak." He shouted over the noisy crowd and motioned to the granite with a frosty, iguana-like digit. "I own the *Broken Wing*."

"Quistix. Is it *that* obvious I'm not local?"

"You're not dressed for the weather here. Plus, I know everyone in Evolt, so…"

Twitch strode up to the other side of the bar and looked around. A pot-bellied barbarian sat and leaned close to a homely woman beside him on a winding tiaga stool. A thin mustache curled out from the top lip of the female barbarian he spoke to. A generous speckling of moles and deep circles under her eyes made Twitch jerk when he saw her. He eyed the woman as he stole from the husky man's coin purse, unable to stop himself from eavesdropping on their argument.

"She's our neighbor, Berlina. She asked for a cup of fat, and I gave it to her. What was I supposed to say?!"

Twitch tucked the coins into his satchel absentmindedly, unable to take his eyes off the woman's jutting teeth. The woman's stunningly low voice made Twitch wonder how someone like her could find someone while he was perpetually single.

"You say, 'My wife wouldn't *appreciate* you coming around!'"

"You've got to be kidding, Berlina. You sound…" He scratched his inch-long beard in annoyance and then toyed with his half-drunk glass of warm ale. His wedding band glinted against his dry, callused finger. For a moment, Twitch wondered if he'd be sly enough to snatch it from the man's mitt without being noticed.

"I looked at her, alright? She's a good-lookin' elf. Is that a crime? You don't see those much up here. It's exotic. You're overreacting. Do you want me to carve out my eyes? It's not like we're gonna elope!"

"You know what?" His wife cried out. "I'm leaving. Enjoy that little pointy-eared bimbo all you want. I'll be in Evolt City with my mother, *thank you very much.*"

Ray growled in frustration and chased her out of the busy room. Quistix and Twitch nabbed the open seats with fervor.

"Unbelievable," Quistix muttered.

"We gotta show out of it, a little *coin*, and look..." Twitch grabbed the two glasses of half-drank ale between them. "Free drinks!" Twitch tossed his back before the semdrog could take it. Frok crept out of her cocoon and yawned.

"No!" Oravak screamed, turning heads. He pointed a scaly finger at the pleom. "You! Get out."

Quistix stood, defensive. "Hey, what's wrong?"

The semdrog pointed to a piece of parchment held to the wall by a nail that read: *No Fire Breathers!*

"You can't be serious," Twitch exclaimed.

"*Deadly.*" Oravak waved to his blue body and white face. "Do you see a single torch in this place? What about a fireplace? Huh?"

Quistix looked around. He was right. She was surprised by the lack of heat inside in such a freezing climate. The beams above them held about fifty jars of lightning bugs, crammed full to provide the dim interior light. "That's why we live in Evolt. We like it cold! That thing needs to *leave.*"

Twitch tried to diffuse the situation. "What if she stays in my bag? You won't even know she is here. I promise... no breathing fire of any kind. And we..." He gulped, holding up newly stolen coins, "shall pay extra for your trouble."

Oravak's eyes squinted, and he shifted his weight uncomfortably. "Fine. But you drink and then leave."

"We're hoping for a room. It's freezing out there." Quistix hoped her persistent stare would crack through his tough shell.

"One platinum." The bartender barked, "And *that thing* stays in the sack."

"One *platinum*? For a room at the Ruby Palace, *maybe,* but in *this* tavern, for *one* night? That's robbery!" Quistix laughed incredulously. "I'll give you ten gold. That's more than fair."

"You can drink. But after, you need to leave." Oravak muttered without any remaining trace of his usual friendly smile.

"Is there another Inn around here?" Quistix sounded hopeful.

"Next one's in Evolt City. It's about a twelve-hour trek from here on foot. Seven by sled."

"Great." Twitch rolled his eyes and seethed sarcasm. "Well, this has been fun."

Twitch winked at a female human sipping brandy next to him. She rolled her eyes and scooted her stool as far away as she could. The wyl scoffed and pulled the loot he'd just taken from the distressed barbarian out of his bag. He pawed through a jingling lump of sovereign silver and slid one across the stone toward Oravak. "Might I trouble you for a glass of muscadine wine before we hit the trail?"

Oravak stared him down for a moment, flipping a cracked toothpick against the smooth sides of his mouth with his elongated tongue. "Muscadines don't grow in Evolt, and we don't get many requests for it, either." He produced a bottle of rich, dark liquid. "We have elderberries around here. Makes great wine."

"I didn't even know you could make wine from elderberries." He managed a weak smile, staring at the delicious-looking contents of the bottle. "I don't even know if I've ever *had* an elderberry."

"Try a sip on the house. You'll love it. You'll want a whole bottle. It's delicious." He poured a dash of the dark liquid into a glass. "The firefly farmer, Leland... his wife, Agatha, makes it right here in Raven Cairn."

Twitch sipped the cold, delectable liquid and smashed a paw-pad hard against the rock slab bar top. "Yes! That is... oh, by the Gods! Fill 'er up! And one for her as well." He slapped two coins on the table. He pushed his glass forward eagerly, and Oravak poured the smooth booze up to the brim and then turned to Quistix. She brushed a ringlet of fiery orange hair from her face, avoiding eye contact with the semdrog.

"So what brings a high elf like yourself to our patch of snowy little tundra?"

"Put another round for them on my tab, Ora." A large barbaric lump of man said next to her. "The young lady's been traveling a long time. She needs a drink. Can't be easy hiding from Exos all these months." He laughed.

Quistix's heart pounded. "What're you talking about?"

"Don't play dumb. We've *seen* the wanted posters. Frankly, most of 'em look like something my daughter, Hilde, would draw, and she's *five*. Loves her charcoal doodles, though. But that last poster the guards started putting up, looks just like ya'. Right down to this 'ere long, fiery ringlet hair 'a yours." He playfully tapped the bottom of one of her dirty curls.

Quistix pushed her stool out and flashed a worried look to Twitch. They needed to leave. *Fast*.

"Now hold on up, little lady. I'm not here to *out* ya'. We ain't fans of the Tempest clan around here. No, ma'am." He laughed and took a swig of mead. "I ain't had nothin' to do with her getting that crown. She's nothing but a spoiled little brat."

"A sadist, she is." The human beside him piped up, dwarfed by the sheer size of his barbarian pal.

"Here in Evolt, we mind our own. What you got goin' on with Exos ain't none of our business." The barbarian said, shoving his empty tankard at Oravak for a refill.

Quistix thought hard for a moment, unsure if she should show her cards, unsure if the man was bluffing. She held up a finger, her tattered fingerless glove fraying. Everything she'd stolen from the Emerald Bandit's den was made with such shoddy craftsmanship. She motioned for the lunking barbarian to lean down. When he did, she extended her hand. "Well, you know my name. Certainly, I should get yours."

She held out her hand to shake, and his belly jiggled with laughter beneath his layered coats. "Samael."

"Thank you for the drink, Samael." Her tone was appreciative. She moved in closer and whispered, "What do you do?"

"I build sleds. Repair 'em. Design new ones. That's how most get around in Evolt. And you, you're a blacksmith, right? One of the best in Bellaneau, legend has it."

"Yes. I was. Well, before some bandit up and... ruined my life." She chugged some of the wine, sadness choking her words a little.

"Sorry to hear that. Hope that bastard gets his."

"He did." She smiled, her citrine eyes glimmering in the light of the firefly jar above him. "Samael, we're trying to find some flying city. Any idea how I can get there?" Quistix set the empty glass onto the bar and licked her chapped, elderberry-flavored lips.

"You mean *Apex*?"

"Unless there's another floating city around here." She panicked, "There isn't, *is there*?"

The barbarian laughed. "No. Just the one. To get there, you have to take the dragon that lives near the *Lush Beaver Inn*. It's about a half day's mush from here by sled. You and your friends can come back to my place and get yourself a hot meal and a bed for the night, and head out in the morning. Wife Lara's a magnificent cook. She's probably already got a big crock of stew boiling." The words made her hungry mouth water. He laughed. "Bed's straw and lumpy, but it's indoors and big enough for all three 'a ya. Getcha a bath and such." He motioned to Oravak, who was tending to another patron. "Won't even charge ya any *platinum,* like this fire-fearin' gouger."

9

*The Raging Infernal Caverns,
Southern Obsidia*

Vervaine sat in the corner of her cell, bruised and bloodied. Dark circles had formed beneath her eyes. She had a reaper's robe wadded up beneath her to protect her from the sharp, unforgiving stone below.

Soul reapers loomed around her cell like a grotesque curtain of flesh, bones, and ichor-spattered fabric. The ruby glow of their eyes had softened. One reached through the bars, and its bony fingers clasped Vervaine's bleeding palm. She caressed what remained of the decayed flesh on its hand and smiled. She looked up at the hooded, torch-lit face in front of her. His teeth were exposed.

His necrotized tissue had turned the pale green of a withering plant, peeling away at the rim of his eyes and nostrils. The reaper took his bony hand and stroked the scarred flesh on her cheek.

Vervaine felt as though she knew what he would ask if only he could form words anymore. "These scars?"

He nodded.

"Well, when I was a girl, there was this little shack just off the palace grounds where the farm tools were kept. It was in terrible shape but adequate. I used to go there to hide. I'd shove my way through the scythes and shovels and burrow myself among the mice and the spiders. Beneath the table of rusty, dust-caked tools, I created a fort and a small straw bed I covered with blankets I stole from the guest quarters. The workers would sometimes spot me. They'd give a polite wave, grab their tools, and scurry out. No one said anything. Some of the workers would leave me little dolls made of dead grass. It was incredibly kind of them, considering how they were treated by my father."

Vervaine paused for a moment as if to prepare herself for her own story. "One day, father and mother had a horrible fight. They were shattering glass. I could hear him throwing her against the stone wall in the next room. I couldn't take it. I went to my shed. That night, Exos followed. After I was inside, playing with my dolls, she locked the door and cast a spell of blaze on the shed. That old, weathered wood went up in flames so fast."

"I remember clawing at the tiny window in the shack and seeing the smile on her face as the smoke tore at my throat. I still have nightmares about the sizzle and smell of my own burning flesh. A flaming board slapped against my skin. I heard the sound of some fracturing wood. I remember being carried out by Omen, and then the world went black. I woke up in agony days later." Vervaine reflexively touched her cheek. "Exos lied and told our father that Omen had set the shack on fire in an act of pyromania. Said *she had seen it with her own eyes.* In return, Father ordered Ceosteol to place a hex on Omen. He would live forever as the embodiment of flame, cursed to burn for eternity."

A distant voice cooed from the cavernous hallways. It sounded familiar. Male. "Ceosteol took away the little tormentor's magical abilities the next day when they found out the truth." The crimson soul reapers parted, allowing Vervaine to see Omen. He appeared in the shadows outside her prison cell. "But, for me, it was too late. *Irreversible,* the old bird said. The first few months were hell. It was… excruciating at first. Then, month after month, decade after decade, the pain dulled. I am numb to it now. I'm numb to nearly everything now."

The words of the hollow man bounced off the bare rock walls as he pressed against the bars. He wanted to reach out to touch her. To comfort her. But that would be out of the question due to his *condition.*

"How are you, old friend?" Vervaine's smile was pleasant. *Nostalgic.* She leaned her head wistfully against the bars.

"I'm well." But his smile was full of pain. He hated seeing her imprisoned there. Exos could be so cruel. "I see all of this hasn't broken your spirit."

"You can break my bones, but breaking my spirit is tougher. I have known love. That is the most spectacular misery of all." Tears welled in her eyes.

"He has been asking about you non-stop." His cobalt eyes were apologetic as blue flames caressed them like lapping waves.

She managed a faint smile. "Thank you." Her voice cracked. She couldn't let the overwhelming darkness inside of her win. She had to stay strong. Arias wouldn't let her rot in this prison.

He would come for her.

"I had a woman once. Before the curse. We were betrothed with plans for a family." His shoulders sagged.

Vervaine felt a sympathetic pain. "*By the Gods.* You've been blamed and suffered all this time."

"I have come to know you well since then, and I know you'd have done the same for me, even knowing the cost."

Suddenly, the infernal caverns felt less harsh and unforgiving than before.

"Master Omen?" The fevered cry of a young man rang out from the dark hallway beyond. "Master Omen? Where did you go?" After a pause, the voice screamed, "Ow! Why are these stones on the floor so sharp?!"

Vervaine smirked, "New recruit?"

Omen nodded and chuckled.

"Did you at least give him boots?"

"He disobeyed a direct order. He doesn't deserve boots." Omen winked at Vervaine, "As you and I have learned through experience, *agony* is not the end of the world."

10

*Samael's Home,
Outskirts of Raven Cairn, Evolt*

In a back room, Quistix sat, half-submerged, in a wooden cask that had been sawed in half and filled with tepid water, made for bathing the barbarian child. The upended top half sat beside it, intended for scrubbing clothes and dishware or for fresh rinse water. Both halves sat below a window, which made baling spent water a cinch. A hunk of snow sat in the second, melting with the heat of the room. Frok burped bursts of fire at it, melting it into fresh, usable water with haste.

In the large main room, the barbarian chased his daughter, Hilde, in circles, occasionally tackling her and roaring like a beast. Her giggles were as shrill as screams. She couldn't be happier. Quistix smiled at the sound of the child's laughter as a tendril of coffee-stained hair fell in front of her face. It reminded her of Danson's laugh. Loud and pure with all the excitement a child could hold.

"Time to rinse! This'll be cold." Twitch said, pouring icy water down her head to wash out the excess coffee. She was a brunette now, her red locks stained dark brown.

The whole house smelled like the beverage, ground and boiled on a kettle over the hearth in the main room. Dying her hair with it had been Samael's wife's suggestion over the hearty stew they shoveled down at the table for dinner.

It wasn't a complete disguise, but it would go a long way now that the new poster had circulated. With brown hair, she'd draw far less attention.

The new poster looked just like her. Finally, it had been a decent likeness. She'd caught a glimpse of it at the *Broken Wing* as Samael ushered them out the door.

"You look rather lovely as a brunette, but I'd be lying if I said I didn't prefer you as a fiery redhead," Twitch added with a smile, rinsing more of the dark fluid out of her soaking mop of tangled curls.

***

Quistix awoke to the blinding light bouncing off the stark white snow outside the bedroom window, refracting into her eyes like the sun through a magnifying glass. For once, she wasn't viewing the peeking sunlight through a mop of messy hair, as Hilde had been kind enough to braid it after her bath.

It was the best Quistix had slept in months, and she dreaded the thought of leaving the warmth of the log home. She could see the charming appeal of living here. There was solitude, vast land, and modest comforts that made life simple and enjoyable, just like where she used to live in Bellaneau– but without all the snow.

She longed to have a place to call her own again. The nomadic lifestyle had never been her forte. She hated wondering when she'd next get to sleep in a bed or have a proper meal. She stretched and shook Twitch.

"Time to get up. We have a lot of hours on foot in this snow. Best go while the weather's nice."

Twitch nodded without a word and groaned as he sat up, nudging Frok's pudgy little body awake.

On a simple desk near the door, there was a pile of clothes along with a note that read:

For Q – With love from Samael, Hilde, and Lara

It was a long-sleeved wool shirt, thick noubald skin leggings, thick knee-high socks, and rugged leather snow boots. Beside it were a large bag of dried elderberries, a wheel of aged cheese, a leather homemade sack canteen of fresh water, and a sack of grain wafer-crackers.

Quistix grabbed the note and wandered out to the main room. Lara was cooking. She wiped her hands on her apron and batted a long strand of black hair from her feminine face. "Perfect timing. We boiled you all some eggs for your journey today."

Quistix held up the note, and tears filled her eyes. "I can't accept this. This is… you're too kind."

"Hogwash. We insist. We have plenty. It's not every day that Samael brings home an outlaw." She smirked. "He headed into town for supplies, but he left you something outside, if you want it. It's not much. Just an old sled he'd repaired for a drunk in town who disappeared and never came to pick it up. We were gonna break it down and use it for firewood, but Sam reckoned you could use it if you had enough money for a dog or two. Get you to where you're going a lot faster than on foot in these parts."

"I don't know what to say." The kindness was choking her up. "I don't know how to ever repay you for all you've done for us."

"We don't need to be repaid. It's the Evolt way. *Help your fellow man.* Or, you know, in your case, your fellow pariah." She giggled.

11

The Wilds of Evolt,
Evolt

Their crunching steps echoed through the snowy landscape as they approached the den. Twitch cupped his hands around his face and squawked like a symph. He repeated the squawk three times. After the third, Aurora's softly glowing velveteen antlers emerged from the darkness. A wash of relief spread over her face.

"'Rora, we got you eldew bew-wees!" Frok said, struggling to hold up the bag of elderberries with her clawed, dragonling stump of a hand.

"I'm so glad to see you. I was worried sick all night that something happened to you." She stared at Quistix's hair and cocked her head.

"I dyed it. With the grounds that we found at the Emerald Bandit's den. You like?"

"It suits you."

"The man we stayed with last night drew us a map to the dragon. Looks like we have a lot of ground to cover. But we had a stroke of luck–" Quistix stepped aside and motioned to the rickety sled. "Ta-dah!"

"Oh, a sled. That's brilliant. But..." She thought for a moment. "Where are we going to find a dog?

"Okay, now hear me out–"

"Oh no, are you kidding?" Aurora circled the sled and looked up at Quistix. "You want me to drag you guys through Evolt?"

Quistix smiled and pressed her hands together. In a begging tone, she said, "It's only for one day. *Pleeeeeease?*"

***

The sled came to a halt, and Quistix jumped off.

"I need a break. We've been at this all day, and I'm exhausted. Frok, can you give me some of those berries? I'm starving." Aurora whipped her head, trying to remove the reins of the sled. Twitch hopped up, pulled the braided rope from around her neck, and tossed it down onto a snow drift.

Quistix studied the map, eyeing the lowering sun's trajectory. The dimming light made the coniferous trees look raven-black along the deep blue mountain. She stepped on a shallow root of a swatting pine and barely missed a swooping branch that swung violently at her.

"Did... did that tree just try to smack me?"

"Yes," Aurora answered, ignoring the aching in her hindquarters. "Swatting pines have a shallow root system with a rubbery core extending through the trunk-like tendons. When pressure is applied to a root, it yanks the branches, and they swat like a reflex."

"Interesting." Quistix nodded, carefully stepping over the next one. "According to Samael's map, we're close."

Ahead, trees cracked and snapped.

A demonic growl rumbled through the valley between elevated peaks peppered with huge swatting pines.

A pair of huge rainbow-colored irises appeared from beneath a pile of snow. The slit pupils readjusted, locking on the travelers.

They blinked.

The mountainous snowdrift before them shook itself off, revealing a hibernating ivory dragon beneath the flaky precipitation. It rose to its feet uneasily, and its color darkened to a vibrant, royal blue. The dragon's wings unfurled, tossed piles of snow off, and extended fully. The dusky sky cast its dim light across its massive sapphire scales and ridges. Snow-white spines stood up from its back and framed its face.

Frok's dewy eyes grew large. She opened her mouth to scream, but no noise came.

Quistix looked back to the others, unsure of what to do. "Do dragons speak a language, Aurora?"

"I... I dunno. Maybe draco-tongue?" Aurora adjusted on her feet nervously and looked for a place to hide if it attacked.

A forked tongue flicked out and retreated back into its scaly mouth. Whirling puffs of smoke billowed from two wide, flattened nostrils. Massive claws jutted from the edges of its wings.

"*Non est tibi... tibi nihil mali ferit.*" Aurora whispered nervously. "Sorry, *mali fecerit.*"

The dragon blinked its eyes sideways. From its chest arose an exhalation of air, like a hearty laugh. Its voice rattled the ground below their feet, vibrating the landscape. "Your draco-tongue is terrible."

"You speak *Destorian*?" Quistix asked incredulously.

"I'm far more proficient at your language than your esteg is at Draco-tongue."

Quistix blinked in amazement and struggled to recompose herself. "Sorry, I'm from Bellaneau. I've never known a proper dragon before, much less one that could speak."

"She didn't get out much," Twitch interjected, trying to sound worldly.

"Frok's the closest thing I've come to meeting a dragon until now." She plucked the pleom out of the pouch. Frok was shaking, and her high-pitched hyperventilating gasps were concerning.

The gargantuan reptile burst into booming laughter, and the earth shook again. Quistix feared it could cause an avalanche from the nearby mountain looming high overhead. After the snow-piled valley stopped shaking, Quistix held the pink, winged ball of trembling blubber to her face and exaggerated her slow breathing, hoping Frok would follow suit. Soon, the dragonling's breaths fell in line with hers.

"It's alright," she cooed and tucked the creature back into the pouch between Aurora's glowing horns. "I'm Quistix. This is Twitch and Aurora. You've already met Frok." She motioned around, attempting introductions. "Do you have a name?"

"Vaynen." He proudly stretched his wings. The creature's sapphire coloring darkened as the sun ducked behind the mountain. The elf's gaze became transfixed on its chameleon-like color-adapting ability.

"It's a pleasure, Vaynen." She smiled genuinely. A stray ringlet of espresso-colored hair fell into her face, bringing with it the faint smell of roasted coffee in the icy air.

"You're the only transport to and from the floating city, right?" Twitch spoke up.

The dragon offered a languid, taxing nod.

"I was afraid you'd say that." Twitch cleared his throat and tried to sound brave. "We need a ride there."

"It's five platinum for the lot of you." Veynan wiggled to find a comfortable position. His barbed tail struck a pine tree, and the spikes wedged deep in its trunk. Annoyed, he tugged the tree from the ground with ease by just the force of his tail. He *thwacked* it on the ground, releasing the barbs and rolling the tree a few yards away with a hissing *whoosh*.

"Five platinum?!" Quistix asked in shock. "Why does everyone in Evolt charge an arm and a leg?"

"I could accept *that* as payment, too." The dragon chuckled loudly, sending several symphs bolting from the pine trees, escaping into the frozen air in panic.

A tiny voice shouted from behind him. "Damn it, Vaynen! How many times do I gotta tell you to lay low and keep quiet? You woke up half of Evolt with that tree smashing!" A hideous goblin in obsidian cotton pants and a noubald leather coat with a mink collar waddled up on squat legs. Quistix guessed he was half her height.

When he saw them, he stopped in his tracks.

"Customers, eh? This time 'a night? Lucky you found us when you did, or you've caught your death." Stomping to the dragon's side in oversized furry boots, he leaned against its sizable thigh.

Quistix cleared her throat. "We need passage to Apex. He said it's 5 platinum."

"5 Platinum? *Vay*, we talked about this! I negotiate, you fly. That's it." He looked out at the travelers and smiled. "For an elf, a wyl, and an esteg… yeah, I'd say 5 platinum."

Twitch ruffled through his satchel, jingling the coins. Counting them.

Quistix sighed, "We don't have nearly enough, sir."

She looked around, genuinely concerned they might freeze to death in the night if they were stranded in such a hostile environment.

Twitch spoke up, his voice ashamed. "Would you take *four* platinum? That's all we have."

As the goblin pondered, Quistix bolted over to Twitch. "Where the hell did you get *four platinum*? Yesterday–"

Her words were halted as she watched Twitch glance back to the dog sled. "I'm sorry."

"Twitch, tell me you're kidding!" Her fists balled. Anger bubbled in her. "You robbed that man after all he did for us?"

"I'm a thief! It's what I do! You haven't minded me pickpocketing anyone else to bankroll this expedition! Why is he any different?"

"He did everything for us! That family went above and beyond. And they had a child!" She growled.

"Half of the men I've stolen from since I met you probably have a child! You don't get to be high and mighty about this when it's convenient for you." He bowed up to her, equally angry. Equally quiet. "You needed money, and I got it. I just saved our lives. You want us to freeze to death out here?! It's not like we have a lot of options for shelter until we can raise more money."

"You didn't know we'd *need* four platinum when you took it. You robbed an innocent man."

"But aren't you glad I did? Huh? This is what it's all been about since we left that bandit den. Do you want to go to Apex or not?"

12

The Skies Above Platinum Cape,
Evolt

Aurora's head rose over the top of Veynan's erect scales. The wind tugged at her horns, brushed past the fur on her face, and dried out her eyes. She was latched tightly with rope to the saddle on the beast. It was the only way since her hooved extremities couldn't clasp on. It wasn't the first time the goblin had lashed an esteg on the dragon, but the last time – years ago – the esteg was headed to Apex as a food source. It was unusual to see one being treated as an equal.

Quistix sat behind the esteg, feet and arms wrapped around as much of the saddle and spinal scale as she could possibly hold. Frok clutched the front of Twitch's billowing fur coat, now soaring like a cape. His spot on the hind end caught the majority of the most powerful gusts. He clenched his sharpened nails into the saddle leather.

Veynan bulleted up at a steep incline, winding through the air with remarkable grace. Its wings flapped with a *whoosh* through the frigid night sky. It broke through the cloud cover and leveled out, cruising smoothly like a shrimping vessel through placid waters.

The colossal mountain ranges of Evolt seemed like inconsequential foothills. Frozen lakes looked like dinky puddles. The world Quistix once knew seemed so unremarkable.

Twitch tapped her shoulder and hollered through the wind, a smile plastered on his furry face. "I know you're angry with me, but I see the smile plastered on your face. Admit it. You *love* this stuff. This sure beats getting drunk in the woods and robbing ewanians all day, doesn't it?"

She hated to admit it. Twitch was *right*. She'd felt more alive in the days of this adventure than she had felt in years. After Danson's death, she'd thought herself dead inside.

But as the bitter cold whipped at her face, she felt very much *alive*.

A smattering of stars shone down, each glimmering with their own story. The three moons seemed larger than ever before, nearly aligned. She was like a child again, without care.

The dragon weaved through the air as though it was carefully stitching into a tapestry made of sky.

Frok gazed up in awe. "Wow," was the only word she could muster.

Holding the rigid saddle handles with a death grip, Quistix looked down. A small cluster of lights in the distance broke through the pitch-blackness. She nodded to Twitch, signaling for him to take in the awe-inspiring aerial view of the city coming into their sights.

Once Aurora noticed what was surely the college towering over the city, her heart leaped in her chest. A long-sought-after wealth of knowledge was finally within reach. Twitch's eyes widened at the sight of the spectacular view below.

A blue-tinged light blazed from several levels of a towering structure cast over the pathways leading to the Institute. Around the building sat four quadrants, divided by cobblestone paths. Different colored lights flickered at the boundaries of the lower right quadrant. Glowing, yellow lanterns hanging from posts were stationed along every path, creating a large, circular outline around the outskirts and lighting the thick, carefully landscaped vegetation growing all over the city. Apex was ovular and pointed at both ends, with pathways carefully created to form the shape of a human eye encased in a circle.

Before they ever touched down in the perfect-looking burgh, Quistix was positive that Apex was a product of magic.

Veynan stopped flapping his wings, landing on an invisible barrier above the street's surface. "*Vivat Hadena.*" The dragon bellowed.

After chanting the words, a lapis streak of light glided over the city in a dome, lighting up its outer boundary. Veynan abruptly fell through the barrier, catching himself before the ground with a single flap of his wings and easing his taloned feet onto the thick meadowgrass.

Warmth washed over them. The climate had abruptly changed from a crisp, freezing breeze to tropically hot as if they'd permeated a hot air pocket. Humidity clung to the glass of the lanterns around the landing pad and gave a fresh, dewy look to exotic flora and fauna. Quistix could've sworn she saw the mouth of a hefty flower snap closed as soon she glanced its way. Its canary-yellow, bulbous head, and smooth stem looked like something Quistix found familiar but couldn't pinpoint.

Veynan's heavy footsteps landed impossibly soft on the spiral cobblestone landing pad. It flattened its body against the platform to make their dismount easier. Eagerly, Twitch clawed his way off of Veynan's shoulder. Quistix untied the rope harness that held Aurora, and they helped each other down. The esteg's legs shook like a newborn.

The path before them was crowded with enormous, rambunctious roses on both sides of the path.

Veynan swiveled. "Welcome to Apex. Be careful not to come too close to any of the plants. They're used for the local alchemist and the college." It nodded toward the northernmost path. "To get to the inn, follow this path a couple miles. It'll be on the left. If you get to the tar pit, you've gone too far."

"Thank you." Quistix's voice was sincere as she stroked the side of the dragon's neck.

Without another word, it flapped its wings and launched back through the skyward climate bubble. Not paying attention, Twitch was thrown off balance by the gust produced by Veynan's wings and fell against the yellow flower. As soon as he made contact, the plant jerked to each side, yanking its massive roots from the soil. Twitch backed away, realizing it was an enormous Timid Tulip.

Frok fluttered from her canopy to the opening in the tulip's head. "Shh, it's otay. He won't hurt you. We's fwendly!"

The tulip lowered its leaves, shaking violently. Frok put her hands on her hips in frustration and dove inside of it head-first.

"Frok!" Aurora clomped to the side of the tulip, looking for an opening. The petals flexed and flicked. From inside, they heard a muffled scream.

Quistix pulled her emerald dagger out of her braided-vine waist-belt and raised it over the flower, ready to slash it to free the dragonling. Suddenly, the petals shuddered and then fell open, exposing two smaller petals toward the center that were tickling Frok mercilessly. She was screaming, alright. Not out of fear. But instead, extreme joy. Quistix lowered the dagger slowly and exhaled a sigh of relief.

"Frok, you get out of there this instant!" Aurora's tone was stern, like a mother chastising her child.

"We was just playeen." Frok's little voice cooed from the center of the flower. Her lip trembled, and her eyes welled up. "You never let me play!"

"Yes, I do! Now come here!"

"I don't gots much time to live, and I don't like bein' yelled at! Especially by a fuddy-duddy like *you*! I hate you, 'Rora!" Frok shot out of the tulip and darted away from the others.

"I know you don't have long. That's why I want to keep you *safe*!" Aurora rounded the corner, hearing Frok's faint weeping in the distance.

Quistix and Twitch followed a forest-like trail lined with foreign plants. A set of blinking eyes cracked open on an inelm tree near the walkway. They followed the crew until they rounded the corner and walked out of view. Aurora scanned the promenade, her ears perking at the sudden high-pitched symphony of symphs howling in the distance.

Quistix couldn't peel her eyes away from the tower that loomed high over Apex. Even from such a far distance, it was a marvel.

13

Whispering Wizard Tavern & Inn,
Apex City,
Apex

The establishment was elegant. Fine coffee-brown tefly leather covered the chair seats and backs, most of which were occupied by elves in vibrant robes. Barmaids walked around, chins high, carefully balancing metal goblets on trays.

Despite the cold, stand-offish stares, candlelight, and red-wood paneled walls made the place feel warm and inviting. Gold-leafed emblems adorned each chair. Crisp, white linens covered the table tops. On each, a golden vase with a bouquet of fragrant wildflowers. The same gold ran along the tops of the walls and along the outer rim of the bar in the back.

Ignoring the judgemental eyes of those around her, Quistix and Twitch took seats at the bar. The same eye emblem they saw hovering above the city was also carved into the front of the bartop, nestled neatly in the middle of swirled, golden embellishments.

Haldir, the slate-gray-skinned bartender, poured the crimson contents of a bottle into a goblet. His pointed, elvish ears poked up through a full head of curly white hair. When he saw them, his eyes widened as if a robbery was imminent.

Quistix tapped her fingers on the blood-wood bar top and spoke quietly, matching the hushed tone of the room. "Got any Muscadine wine?"

The bartender shrugged and looked at Twitch, who tossed his satchel to the floor by his hind paws.

"Or elderberry?!"

"Please lower your voice!" Haldir chastised with a whisper, setting a bottle down. The tavern shifted into silence, every pair of eyes on them. Many gazes were frightened, some angered, and the rest disgusted.

"We do not carry peasant swill, much to your disappointment, surely. And we don't serve *his* kind here."

"Are you serious?" Quistix responded with an edge to her voice, offended. She tried to rein in her temper.

Twitch had followed Haldir's frightened expression to Quistix's blazing, white eyes glowing with outrage.

"How much for just a room, then?" She flexed her jaw.

"A room here is out of the question for the likes of you." Haldir's voice was curt.

Quistix imagined punching him in the face so hard that his teeth would embed in the back of his skull. "By the *Gods*, what is your issue with us?"

"My issue is with *you*." He spoke quietly, readjusting his black cotton robe. "I saw your eyes. You were born with magic. Between your clothes and your less-than-savory companions, it's clear you've squandered your gift. People like myself have to work, study, and practice every day just to hone our skills. I have no pity or patience for an elf who turns their back on their inherent abilities when the rest of us kill ourselves to achieve it. I rest three hours a night to work enough for tuition to a school that promises to make me like *you*. From where I stand, your gift has done you no favors."

Quistix pressed both hands flat to the table. "I was raised by a blacksmith on a floundering farm with poor soil in Bellaneau. I had no knowledge of my abilities until recently. You judge without knowing a single thing about me. Why? Because I smell? Because I wear shoddy clothes? Because I never *knew* I could be more than a mother and blacksmith? You have no idea what I've been through to get here."

"I think it's time you leave, madam." Haldir pointed to the ornate gold-emblemed entry doors.

"Is there another inn around here? Perhaps one where the person running the place isn't a judgemental elf who's failed himself in his life and wants to take it out on others who just need a roof over their head for a night?"

"Afraid not." He said with a wicked grin creeping up onto his taut, elven skin.

14

*The Raging Infernal Caverns,
Southern Obsidia*

Exos strode in like a woman on a mission. As she rounded the corner into Vervaine's cell, the mad quichyrd was petting an odorous, tailed infernal's mangy fur. Fur that sloughed off with every loving stroke of her bony, feathered talons. The queen watched the gruesome display of affection in utter disgust.

Exos kneeled before a figure swathed in bloody wrappings. As she pulled the cloth from skin, she recognized the mangled body.

Vervaine.

Or rather, *what was left of her.*

The cooling corpse had a clearly dislocated shoulder. The arm akimbo, gnarled fingers brushing the slashed skin of her hip. Claw marks crusted with dried blood. One of her legs was broken. *Twisted.*

Omen stood reverently in the corner beyond the quichyrd. Arms crossed. Flames silently lapped up his face like a sea of wrathful waves. He stared at the corpse of the girl he'd watched grow into a kind, loving woman. One he was eternally cursed for protecting. For once, the pain he felt *physically* was overridden by emotional agony.

She always thought her sister's death would come as a relief, but instead, she felt hollow and empty. Joy was overridden by disbelief. Exos looked to the devastated crimson soul reapers locked in their magically-fortified cell.

They'd gone too far.

"What happened here?" There was no emotion but rage in Exos' voice, which stunned even Omen. Her callousness knew no bounds.

"The crimson soul reapers did what you ordered Nictis to teach. *Torture*. That's what you wanted, wasn't it? To make your sister feel every ounce of pain she could because she had the affection you craved?" Ceosteol never took her eyes off the corpse.

"I was trying to teach her a lesson. Not *murder* her, you twat!" She growled into the air and then bared her teeth at the tailed infernals. "I knew all of these anathemas of yours and Nictis' were *trash*!" Exos kicked the water pail on the floor, sloshing pink-stained fluid across the jagged crystal floor, serrated like a knife's edge.

"Watch your tongue!" Ceosteol warned. "You may hold a title, but these *infernals* are part of my *soul*." Ceosteol tried to hide her offended tone by pressing her beak against the snout of one of the dual-headed beasts. It graciously lapped at her with two eager, rotten tongues slithering out of its heads like some zombified canine science experiment.

The second head of the infernal attacked the first out of bitterness and envy, clamping both sets of bone-exposed jaws and snarling ferociously. The remaining hackle-hair on its necks stood on end.

"*Audite sermonem meum et cessate!*" Ceosteol shouted.

The green, whirling smoke in their eyes grew brighter, and both infernals sat upon their snake tails. Their many faces turned toward her, awaiting a command.

"Wake her!" Exos demanded, still partially in denial. As if she could order her sister to live again. As though she was so used to getting her way that she could defy even death itself with her stubborn aggression. *But she couldn't.*

Ceosteol kneeled beside the body and stared at the queen, eyes glowing green orbs in her hollowed-out sockets. "There's no waking her. Vervaine is dead."

Exos nearly fell. Her head was light, her lungs weak, unable to gasp enough air. She hunched over, unsteady. The world spun. She pounded her closed fists against her temples with increasing intensity, rapping her knuckles hard against her skull. She screamed shrilly and coughed violently, speckling her sister's body with specks of ruby fluid.

The soul reapers grew frenzied with pleasure at her tortured bellows.

"You defiant little *bitch*!" The last word was venomous. *Hateful*. She kicked her sister's limp body in the ribs. The bones snapped. The rigor made her tough flesh unforgiving.

Exos heard her own heartbeat in her ears. "*Bring her back.* This whole thing was just supposed to put her in her place. Not kill her. My orders were *implicit*."

Ceosteol cackled at the nerve of the woman above her. Always *taking*. Promises perpetually crumbling. And now she wanted *another* favor. The feathers on the back of her neck stood on end, life force whooshing angrily through her cold-blooded veins. She stood, unwavering. Didn't move a muscle, just stared with those glowing balls of green light casting a neon haze across the smooth surface of her toucan-like beak.

"The reapers don't know when to stop. They feed off pain and misery, and you gave her a lot of it." Omen interjected, arms still tight across his chest.

Exos kept her eyes trained on the quichyrd, ignoring Omen's blame. "Do it! I've seen how much you *love* to tinker with all of your little dead things. Here's another one. Just like you did to those poor wyl children all those years ago. *Do it to her*!" She screamed.

"I'm tired of being used by you," she squawked, "year after year with hope dangling like a carrot just out of reach. You're *cruel*. You always *were*, even as a *girl*. I'm done doing your dirty work. I've done as you asked. I helped *make* you queen. I helped *keep* you queen. Everything you *are* and *have* is because of *me*!"

"I ought to slit your throat right here and feed you to those rotten abominations!"

"Do it! *Kill me now,*" she breathed deep, "or sign my pardon. Hand it off to your men. Clear my name. Only *then* will I soul-bond her to me."

"All you ever talk about is the pardon! Your incessant begging is maddening! You know I can't actually pardon you. The fact that you keep falling for it tells me how much of a *fool* you are!" The room grew totally silent. "Am I to grant *all* prisoners their freedom? Or just the crazed quichyrd who experimented with wyl children? The twisted witch who stitches together wild animals? The one who creates these... undead *abominations.* You *really* think I can pardon a monster and the Destorians will let me *keep my throne*?"

"Yes! You have always done what you wanted, no matter the fallout, you little *brat*! This is no different. I've *earned* this!" The quichyrd spread a wing toward Vervaine's body. "If I do this, she won't be the same, which I know will please you *immensely.* I'd be creating another extension of myself, just like *them*." She ruffled a wing toward the tailed infernals, sitting obediently at her feet. "In your eyes, she'll be *better*. Passable for public addresses. I can make her *say* and *do* anything you want." Her serious expression curled into a grin. "But she doesn't walk the streets again... until *I do*."

15

The Streets of Apex City,
Apex

"This seems like as good a place as any." Quistix pointed to a cobblestone alley just off the city's main courtyard. There were piles of rubbish heaped in a stack near the left wall.

Behind them stood a massive granite statue of a mage, his hands splayed before him. He appeared to be in the middle of turning a rakaaby into a human. Graceful ribbons of stone swirled around the floppy-eared morphing creature. Aurora couldn't take her eyes off of it.

"Fine by me," Aurora said, enamored with the stonework. "I'm used to sleeping outside."

"At weast it's *warm*!" Frok exclaimed from her hammock, picking her teeth lazily with a piece of splintered wood.

Twitch dropped the pile of sticks he was carrying – treasures of the trek, as he'd called them – and grabbed a sack of trash. He hurled it into a corner with a grumpy scowl and kicked it once, for good measure, before lounging against it like a lumpy sack of grain.

"Living the high life, once again." He grumbled and snatched up the sticks. He started running his blade across them. Creating arrows often helped soothe his frustrations. It was a relaxing activity for him.

"It's just for a night. Tomorrow, bright and early, we will go to the Institute, and I'll see what I can do to get us a better place to sleep while we're here.

"Why? This is great!" The wyl's voice was thick with sarcasm. "This place smells great. Cushy bed. Great view." He stared over at the overflowing dumpster, thick with flies. "Five-star accommodations, madam."

16

Institute of Magic,
Apex City,
Apex

The witch looked up to see a rounded stone building standing tall and proud above a wall of shrubbery. Gray, stone gargoyles sat perched at the top, their carved eyes watching every direction. The windows were arched, sandwiched between stone pillars. Between them stretched swirling semi-transparent indigo-tinted barriers of magic. As the morning light poured through them, they looked like stained glass walls. The outer stonework dividing each floor had Destorian and Latin words for different types of magic.

A jagged piece of earth arose from the soil behind the shrubs. Roots and dirt hung down like jellyfish tendrils from the grassy platform. On it were three students of magic in their 20s, each with an armful of books. The platform rose along the side of the building, stopping at the third story. They walked through the transparent force field and disappeared.

An elf with sapphire eyes and pale, yellowed skin exploded out of nothingness into their field of view. Two more bursts of light produced armored mages in polished brass armor, their staffs crossed in an "X." Their cuirasses were etched with the encircled-eye insignia. Arcs of blue electricity connected the tips of the staves like a blinding, steadily-striking lightning bolt.

A scrawny, elven student was pushed out through the barrier, landing on his overstuffed suitcase. He dusted himself off, walked up to the guards, and attempted to regain entrance to the front hall. He was halted in place by the sentinel's crackling staves, alive with the surging magic between them. The boy's blue robe clung to his sinewy frame, and a yellow sash jerked around his waist as he threw his hands up in protest of the denied entry.

"Kick me out?! *Me*?! It wasn't a big deal! Do you know who I am? My parents paid for the entire *Healing Ward*! Forget this stupid school!" The student screamed and then headed down the pathway straight toward the ensemble of travelers. Twitch ducked behind a bush, but Quistix stood tall, unable to break her gaze.

"Professor Daetumal wouldn't have overreacted like this!"

Quistix raised her eyebrows when she heard the name.

"Don't be surprised if you two find yourselves out of a job!" He huffed and stormed away.

Quistix approached the guards brazenly. She didn't have a plan. She rarely formulated one, instead acting on pure gut instinct.

"Excuse me, gentleman." Quistix nodded reverently at the guards as a sign of respect. "How might someone like myself gain access to the Institute?"

The men eyed her up and down but didn't say a word.

"What is your business with the Institute?" A feminine voice arose from within the face helm of the guards. A jarring revelation, as Quistix had assumed them to be men based purely on their size and stature.

Quistix looked to Aurora. "We've traveled a long way. My friend wishes to read from your library."

The guards looked at one another, holding as still as the gargoyles above. One finally spoke. The male. "I'm sorry, ma'am. Only students, staff, and relatives beyond this point."

"Well, coincidentally, if I just heard that boy right, it sounds as if I'm related to a professor here. Would that qualify?"

"Who is your relative?" His voice sounded distrustful.

"Professor Daetumal." Quistix answered uneasily.

"And your name?" The other guard asked.

Quistix thought for a moment. She was a wanted woman, and giving her name could lead Exos' guards right to her. She might as well hand herself over on a silver platter. After some soul-searching, she spoke. "Quistix Daetumal."

"Why does that name sound so familiar?" The male asked the female.

"I've heard that name before."

Twitch gulped, and Quistix's heart leaped into her throat. They had surely seen the bounty posters, her moniker emblazoned in bold font across the top.

This was it, she thought.

The two guards whispered to each other before finally nodding. The woman spoke this time. "We require proof. Can you verify this?"

Quistix thought for a moment, wracking her tired, weary brain for a way to prove herself. Then, it came to her with an "aha" bolt of brilliance. She hurried to the esteg, reached inside the poorly designed saddlebags they'd made, and produced her book. She unwrapped it from its ewanian leather pouch and opened the front cover.

The guards stood together over the ancient-looking tome and read the inscription:

To my daughter, Quistix,

You are alchemy incarnate. From afar, I've watched you grow, and I am so proud of you. May enlightenment illuminate your path and guide your footsteps.

Love, Eldrin Deutumal.

The handwriting was neat and tidy, and each letter was almost the exact same height and distance from the next. Quistix had read it dozens of times, never fully understanding what it meant.

"We need to check with the Headmaster. Please wait here."

Quistix reflexively reached out to grab her father's book, but the guard who held it had already spun around on her heels and marched across the main hall. Together, the guards clattered up a wide, winding staircase.

Awash with a mixture of concern and confusion, Quistix turned and flashed Aurora a weak, reassuring smile. If this worked, it meant the end of their journey together. She'd done what she'd set out to do, and the esteg's life would be wildly enriched from it.

The quick *clomps* of metal guard boots neared, thundering against the marble floors.

A sleek, platinum-haired elf followed the guard and shoved past her with a welcoming grin and wide-open arms. Her crimson irises softened. She wrapped her arms around Quistix and hugged her tightly. "Oh my, how you've grown!"

Quistix was speechless.

"Oh, where are my manners? You probably don't even remember me. I'm Madam Emma Aerendyl, Headmaster of the *Institute of Magic.* Though I was just a student here when I saw you last. That feels like eons ago." She laughed, a tinge of nervousness seeping into her tone. She fidgeted with the long sleeves of her pristine robe. "I'm so pleased to see you've made your way back after all of these years. I–" She hesitated, stumbling on the way she wanted to phrase the next sentence. "I... I'm so sorry for your loss."

Quistix's mood darkened. She cocked her head, staring quizzically. "What loss?"

The Headmaster gasped and clasped her mouth.

"No one told you?" Madam Aerendyl exhaled long and hard and swept the Institute's courtyard with her eyes. "I'm so sorry, Ms. Daetumal, your father passed away nearly a month ago. An awful accident in his laboratory. I'm so sorry you had to come all this way to find out."

Quistix stuttered, "I... I didn't really *know* him. Just a few faint memories." Her mind swam with images, questions, memories, and overwhelming feelings of loss for someone she barely knew.

"It's perfect that you're here. We have some matters to discuss about his possessions. If you would please follow me." Headmaster Aerendyl started inside. Not hearing Quistix's footsteps follow, she spun around. "What's wrong?"

"I'm actually not here about my father." Quistix gestured to the esteg, "Aurora traveled all the way from the Bramolt mountains to visit your library. We've been traveling for weeks, barely eating, sleeping wherever we can to get her here. She has a thirst for knowledge, and the college library here is second to none, so we've heard."

"It is. Unfortunately, we don't allow non-relatives of faculty or students to enter." Headmaster Aerendyl tucked a loose strand of silver hair back into her braid and stared apologetically. "However, your father was a *legend* here. And he would be furious to know that I turned you away. Out of respect to Eldrin, *Gods rest his soul*, I believe I am willing to make an exception." She flashed a shy grin and cleared the path, welcoming the weary travelers inside. The guards pressed to either side of the entryway, lowering their staves. The electricity between them fizzled. Aurora nodded to each guard as she passed through. Frok's eyes bulged at the sight of the main hall.

***

Headmaster Aerendyl led the disheveled explorers through the great main hall of the administration building, beneath the winding staircase, and out a set of double doors to another breathtaking courtyard on the other side. Beyond a tall herb garden sat a massive bridge arching high in the sky. As they trekked, Quistix peered over the stone walls of the bridge, eyeing infinitesimally small white-capped waves of a churning sea of water far, far below.

This truly was a floating city. Hunks of pristine, manicured flora-laden land were connected by sky-bridges hanging miles over Platinum Cape. If she squinted, she could see small, dark blips on the water. Shipping vessels traveling through the treacherous seas of Destoria.

Before Aurora could protest, Frok launched from her cocoon and fluttered over the edge, half a mile down toward the frenzied waters below. The warm air in Apex, mixed with its perfect blue sky, made her shout with glee, her tiny voice echoing back at her from the rocks of the bridge. Aurora told her, many times, that legend has it that no pleom had ever made it to Apex before. Elated, she soaked in the view of the wide waves lapping far below. Being the first of her kind was such an honor.

This is the kind of adventure she'd always dreamed of.

Magical walls, floating cities, and dragons were all a part of a world she never thought she'd survive long enough to see.

Seeing the looks of wonder on their faces, the Headmaster raised her slender hands. With a flourish, gorgeous mandevilla vines crept quickly through the crags and divots of the rock wall, separating them from the walkway and the perilous fall. Magenta flowers blossomed throughout the vine, peppering the gray stones with vibrant bursts of vivid color. Twitch's mouth hung open at the sight of such a wonder. He understood why Apex was so perfectly landscaped. With power like that, it would be simple to maintain a botanical oasis.

At the end of the bridge, two elven guards sat on each side of the massive brass gate, and another stood with perfect posture in the middle, his armor blinding in the summer-like sun.

Madam Aerendyl held her hands together in the air and moved them apart slowly, her ruby-red eyes closed in concentration. Her enchantment spread the massive gates open wide, and the elf in the middle stepped to his right dutifully to allow them passage.

Beyond the gates sat a small, lush courtyard with precisely organized stones and vining plants thriving, intertwined, swirling up tall trellises on every side. Polished stone steps circled a building, and on the far side, four sets of carved wooden doors stood forty feet high at its entrance. Students walked in and out of the doors, each opening them with mental, effortless magic, their arms stuffed with daunting piles of textbooks.

"Welcome to the *Institute of Magic*." Madam Aerendyl walked in first, spinning and widening her arms like she was showing off a gallery full of fine art. "Home to 183 students of magic and 37 highly-revered members of staff."

In the center of the lobby thrived a circular garden with a pond in the center. Butterflies, bees, and fairies fluttered around the magically-enclosed biosphere of bustling life. Several gold-scaled fish breached the surface of the water, mouths emerging for only a second or two before dipping beneath again.

Two marble benches in the biosphere were occupied by elven students in colorful robes, their bare feet dangling in the pond alongside the fish.

"Magic can be draining. We've provided a garden of sorts for the students to recuperate from their course load. Students are magically charged differently, each requiring one of the four natural elements to draw from. This central garden is off-limits, hence the biosphere dome. It has the dual function of providing us with a variety of plants for our alchemy classes."

Quistix perked up at the word alchemy, the very term bringing back some of her only positive childhood memories with her grandfather.

Indigo forcefield-filtered sunlight flooded through windows evenly spaced around the room. Columns stood proudly, encircled with winding grape vines and a colorful array of trumpeting morning glories. Floating orbs of light, tucked into overgrowths of ivy on the walls, cast warm light in the darker spaces. A wide spiral staircase wound high overhead to the top floor, several stories up. Madam Aerendyl led them above.

"This level is for the study of *Illusion*." A smattering of students stood in different-colored circles in a vast room with mind-bogglingly tall ceilings. "This course is for the basics. As you may see from the age of those students, they are all just growing into their magic. In a few years, they'll be capable of creating entire landscapes and manipulating all five of the senses."

An elvish girl with long, blonde hair and garnet eyes brushed past them, put down her books, closed her eyes, and stood in silence near the railing in the middle. In her hand, she held a stemless, rambunctious rose nearly the size of her head. Twitch's whiskers fluttered as he watched her trace a circle on the stone floor around herself with her foot. Suddenly, where her foot had been, a fiery red line appeared. She dropped the flower head, and the design of the Institute's eye-insignia appeared vibrantly in red light in the circle. Her eyes opened. They were completely red, sclera-and-all, both laser-focused on the de-stemmed flower.

She jerked her wrist, and the flower flipped, standing up on its petals. A wave of her hand, palm up, and the rose floated up like a brilliant-red jellyfish swimming toward the surface of the ocean with tentacle-like petals, swirling as it changed direction, fluttering overhead.

The rose's color drained, quickly overtaken with dulled shades of gray. Decomposing in an instant, it crumbled to ash and fell, like dust, to the floor.

A one-eyed ewanian pushed a bristly broom over and swept up the rose. He forced a smile at them from the stair platform, his sagging air sac shaking like loose chicken fat with every movement.

They carried on up another long, winding flight to the next story. Quistix regretted the lengthy tour already, her thighs maddeningly sore from straddling Veynan's huge, rattling saddle the day prior. They collectively halted on the landing, staring in at an impossibly large room, nearly identical in shape to the one prior.

Dozens of students stood before enchanting tables. Indigo light whirled around blades of daggers, floating necklaces, and spinning rings. Every student chanted in Latin, pounding the sides of the table with crystals in each hand, sending bolts of electricity into the air.

"This is the level of *Enchantments*. Assignments are based mostly on protection, healing, and destruction. Curses are strictly prohibited." The Headmaster's smile faded. "If any black magic is witnessed on these premises, those involved will be expelled and ejected immediately. The floors are made of agate, as is every floor above. We had it mined and imported for the stone's properties. It promotes the safety of our students, thus the name *safety stone*."

"The student that was escorted by the guards earlier, past the gates... was that an expulsion?" Twitch sounded curious.

"Indeed." She replied, the weight of her words heavy. "Come, there's still much to see."

17

*The Raging Infernal Caverns,
Southern Obsidia*

A portal opened on the wall, and Ceosteol entered through it. It was an exhausting spell, but it would allow her to get Vervaine to her dank, underground lair without sounding alarm bells with anyone who spotted them.

Once inside, she set the body down and faced the door carved into the exposed dirt and clay walls of her underground sanctuary. With a flourish of her wing, the portal sealed, and the edge around it disappeared as if it never existed. She hoped she had enough energy left. The physical and magical exertion taxed her ancient body.

She scurried down the steps. Hands trembling, she scrambled for supplies. In the near-darkness, she ambled over to shelves of glass jars and metal containers, squinting to read her own handwriting. Unable to decipher the labels, she ignited a wall torch with a woof of emerald fire at just the flick of her frail wrist.

After carefully selecting three large vials, she poured the contents of each into a glass pickling jar on her alchemy table. The first was a pungent, black, tar-like sludge that *glopped* from its glass container. Dikeeka had many uses, though its original design was for far more *nefarious* creations such as this. Its noxious odor clung to the air long after the cap had been replaced.

Next, she held a bottle of smoking yellow liquid. As she popped the cork from the top, a bright flash made her see spots, and a small ball of fire erupted and dissipated, filling the room with an odorous, charred stench. She poured it quickly and replaced the cork.

Cautiously, she held the last vial in her hand. *Warm to the touch.* Within the teal liquid encased in the glass, she watched as memories from her life swirled in colorful stripes through the blue sludge. *Her essence of being.* Painfully extracted through the years for purposes such as these. She poured it atop the other components.

In the liquid, as she stirred with a wooden spoon, she heard her voice as a child, begging her to stop. The chilling cry made her feathers stand erect. She smelled the scent of the lavender field beside her childhood home in Silvercrest, followed by her mother's Asyrian perfume.

She placed a cap on the pickling jar and shook the concoction against the glass like a maraca, watching as the color shifted to the same haunting green as her eyes. Her gaze wandered to the nook beside the stairway.

Vervaine's body.

Bruised, battered, and broken.

She opened the elf's cold lips with sharp talons and poured the contents of the jar in, grinning at the thought of walking free in Destoria once again. Free to go anywhere, see anyone she wanted, gather supplies, and experiment as she pleased.

18

The Institute of Magic,
Apex City,
Apex

"I believe you might enjoy the next few levels in particular," the Headmaster said, smiling at the esteg as she trotted alongside her. Aurora nodded excitedly, clacking her feet against the stone floor with uneasiness and excitement as they reached the plateau. "This is the *Restoration* floor. Seeing a living esteg will be a real treat for the students. Here, we specialize in curing common maladies. They work closely with the professor to practice healing spells and wards of protection. One day, we hope to provide all of Destoria with our healing capabilities. Just like on the sister isle,

Asera, where healing magic is common practice. We are here to heal, never to harm." Gesturing to the occupied beds beside the staircase, she continued. "Today, due to a misfire of unsupervised magic after casting hours, several of our students are being tended to, as you are about to see."

They watched as a male student in a long sapphire-blue robe stood silently, hood up, beside the bed of a large, badly burned barbarian girl in her teens. Quistix saw the young man's brown curly hair and thought of Danson, imagining him as the grown student. She smiled at the fantasy of her child being able to grow up and explore his gifts and future.

The wounded barbarian's hair was streaked with soot, and several patches melted together. The healer's hands stretched over her body as cerulean tendrils of magic spiraled down from his flexed fingers into her abdomen. The reddened, exposed flesh mended her slowly until there was no longer a wound.

"Headmaster," a weak voice called out several beds away.

Madam Aerendyl excused herself and walked to the elven student. His slate-gray eyes were surrounded by reddened sclera, and the shade of his nose seemed to match. His hands were bandaged, and his pale yellow face was charred badly. She grabbed a tin cup from the wooden stand by his bed and lifted it to his lips. He sipped the water and nodded for her to take it away.

Twitch realized many of the teenagers in the room had similar burns.

"This is why black magic is strictly forbidden. It's dangerous. *Volatile*. No good can come of it. Once these students heal, they will serve as a living example to the magic community on the dangers of black magic." She patted the young man on the hand and leaned in. After a hushed exchange, she walked back to the stairwell, eyes pained.

The next floor brought them to an enormous library. Students sat on benches by the handrails, reading feverishly. Five stories high, it had books stacked floor-to-ceiling along every wall. Tall, unsteady towers sat by chairs, needing to be sorted and returned to the shelves. There were no windows on this level, but it was lit brightly by scattered orbs of light. Dozens of orbs hovered in the center of the room like a massive chandelier.

"These ancient texts are incredibly delicate. To have windows in here would be unwise. In fact, many students have to wear gloves to touch the ones stored in the side rooms behind the shelves. Only Professor Patteryl and his assistant Annabelle have permission to grant students access."

Aurora stepped closer, eyes glimmering with tears. It was the most beautiful sight she'd ever witnessed.

"We have the largest, most comprehensive library in all of Destoria. Some of these old scrolls and drawings would rattle Destoria's foundation."

"Headmaster Aerendyl, pardon my forwardness, but might I stay and study here at the college?" Aurora asked politely. "My hooves would never touch the books, and Frok's hands are so small you'd never know she touched them. It has been my dream for a lifetime to drink in the wealth of knowledge between these walls."

"I'm afraid that is not possible." As the words left Madam Aerendyl's mouth, Aurora felt the crushing weight of her dreams being shattered. "You are not a student, faculty, or a relative of either. This area is off limits for study otherwise."

Quistix spoke reluctantly, "If I enrolled to become a student, might she stay?"

Madam Aerendyl looked at Quistix. "This college has rules that have been here long before me and will be around long after. I've been lenient on account of your father, but the rules state if she is not family, then after this tour, she must leave. Even if you somehow came up with the two hundred platinum per semester, you would not be above the rules."

Twitch nearly fainted at the steep price tag.

Quistix stepped closer, her tone pleading. "I stand before you as a woman with nothing left to lose. We are two different sides of the same sovereign coin. Maybe you were born here, or you've been groomed for this position for years. I doubt you've ever had to watch your whole life burn before your eyes. We've traveled across Destoria, surviving azure shifters and bandits, sleeping outside, scavenging for food and coin, and wiping out our purses, flying to a floating city where we've been greeted with judgment… just to get her here. And now you're turning her away? I'm begging you to allow her access. She simply wants to read. You would want the same for someone you cared for, would you not? Someone who had a thirst for knowledge. Just like you did for your son down there in the burn ward."

The Headmaster's eyes enlarged, but Quistix continued gently.

"I saw the way you held his hand. How he called to you. I used to have a son, Headmaster." She cleared her throat, trying to reel back her emotions. "I know the bond of a mother and son when I see it."

Madam Aerendyl stared into Quistix's piercing tangerine-toned irises, unsure what to say. "Since you have a notable mystical lineage, I can grant you a two-week scholarship on the grounds of who your father was and how much he meant to all of us. But as far as you are concerned, Aurora, I'm sorry, but the rules are in place."

Aurora clomped against the stone steps toward her, nudging Quistix gently aside with her head.

"How about a battle of wits instead? If I answer all of your questions correctly, then you give me access to the library for the two weeks she's enrolled. If I fail even one answer, I'll leave willingly right now."

Madam Aerendyl was intrigued. She tapped a pointer finger against her lips and smiled. "Why are the fish of the Glitter Gulf reflective?"

Without thought, Aurora eagerly responded, "According to the ewanian text 'Willowdale: an Omnibus" by Franz Ordenlacht, a curse was cast over the lake after a mage was bitten by a sharp-toothed fish as he bathed in the darkness to hide his deformities from prying eyes. Thus, the curse was cast so he might see them in the dark during future baths. However, scientifically, the truth is that the coloration comes from an evolutionary, adaptive deformity caused by persistent pollution of the gulf."

"Alright, I must admit that was a bit impressive." The Headmaster rocked on her heels. "How does Apex remain the floating city?"

Yet again, the esteg throttled her with a rapid-fire answer. "It floats due to a masterful suspension spell cast by a minimum of three experienced mages at once. It must be recast every week. However, during your father's reign as Headmaster, he had called a meeting of his council on a day of renewal, and Apex descended hundreds of feet in an hour."

The Headmaster smiled broadly. "Sing to me the song of Apex, *but in inelm tongue.*"

"*Aked ure dkis pers-*" Aurora said before being interrupted by the Headmaster's laughter.

"Alright! Cedrick isn't even that well-versed in inelm, and he's our *ambassador*. You're obviously well-educated. Where have you studied?"

"The monk's temple of the Bramolt mountains. It was the only other scholarly library in Destoria."

"How do you read with no hands?"

Aurora looked up to the hammock between her antlers and shook it. Frok clasped her hands around the rim of the fabric and peeked out.

"Hi!" She squeaked. "I holded the books for her."

The Headmaster chuckled. "A pleom and esteg working in tandem. I've read about it but never witnessed it for myself. Extraordinary.

The Headmaster's face reddened with embarrassment. "I'm happy to approve your request."

19

Ceosteol's Underground Cavern,
Amethyst Cove,
Obsidia

Old blood stained the dirt floor. Bottles shimmered along the shelves, their contents in a spectrum of colors ranging from neons to swirling black oils.

Vervaine's electric-green eyes shot open. Lurching up, she sputtered blood violently until she cleared her lungs. She pulled her knees to her chest and swatted the air as if viewing wild hallucinations. Her day-glo eyes intensified, and she erupted in an ear-piercing scream. The jars in Ceosteol's lair exploded, and the modest straw bed caught fire.

A wicked smile crept onto the quichyrd's face, and a sick sense of relief filled her at the necromanced corpse gasping for air before her.

It worked.

20

Institute of Magic, Conjuration Level,
Apex City,
Apex

A wispy, semi-transparent eagle flew past, tousling Quistix's coffee-dyed hair. Dozens of translucent animals, ranging from wolves to ferrets, bustled throughout the room in response to the students' spells, each standing within their own circle, intensely focused on their craft.

"This is the level of *Conjuration*," Aerendyl announced proudly, waving at Professor Glenshire. The old woman smiled and waved back before tending to another student.

"These are projections. Soon, students will learn to conjure weapons for defense as well.

Conjuration, while a very useful skill set, is a challenging subject. These are novice-level students. Those *majoring* in conjuration will learn to summon things that are more advanced, like modes of transportation and shelters for inclement weather."

An opaque esteg waltzed toward Aurora, touching its nose to hers before dissipating into smoky oblivion. The bashful elvish student behind it watched from across the room. Light eyebrows framed her mead-colored eyes.

Quistix explored the room on the next floor with great interest. With no students in class, she wandered, weaving through the marred alchemy tables, dragging her fingers across the burned tabletops, inspecting various beakers and jars lining floating shelves. She inhaled deeply, savoring the familiar smell of wildflowers and herbs. Quistix's gaze became transfixed on a jar of butterflies.

A memory from long ago struck her with a bewitching force. She was a young elf in the recollection, no more than four. Her father scurried around this room after she set a jar of monarch butterflies free. The act was intentional. That she remembered, too. She wanted to help them escape this place. She giggled as her father leaped through the air, swiping at fluttering insects with empty glass jars.

Madam Aerendyl approached, chuckling. "I was just an assistant here when you were born. Your father was my favorite to work for. His classes were always wildly entertaining. He would bring you often. It absolutely *killed* your father to send you away. Pardon the poor choice of words." Her eyes softened. "After your mother passed, he was never the same. It was as if the light in his eyes was snuffed out."

Quistix headed toward the stairs, eager to get away from the memories. Madam Aerendyl watched her walk away, struck with a strong pang of sympathy for the lost elf. "We should hasten our pace. I must get back soon. I've got meetings with the parents of the infirmed."

Side by side, they walked to the next floor, the others following closely behind. Stepping up to the next level, they arrived at the teacher's dormitory. Instead of an incredibly expansive area as with the floors before, it was a single, narrow, two-person hallway with tall, slim dorm doors only a few feet apart. Each had a name carved into the wood along with the symbol for their school of magic.

"The next two floors are for the teachers, the one after is the dining hall, and, lastly, the four floors above that are student dormitories. The building where I met you holds the student council chambers, a formal dining hall, and my office. Please do not hesitate to come find me there."

Fourteen doors down the narrow hall, the Headmaster stopped. The door had a vial and a phoenix carved into it. The name scrawled neatly into the wood read:

Professor Eldrin Daetumal.

Madam Aerendyl removed a large ring of keys from the pocket of her robe and shuffled through them, talking to herself. "Kitchen, Library, Library, Janitorial, Office, Library, Professor Natelson... ah! Here we go. *Daetumal.*"

The space was thin, walls tall, floor narrow like an alleyway shooting deep. One entire wall was just a massive bookshelf with its own curated library overflowing with alchemy and restoration books, requiring a sliding ladder to reach the top tiers. Alternating banners depicting blue phoenixes and orange vials hung along the opposite long wall from the books.

"Here is your humble abode for the next two weeks." She swirled a teacup half-full of moldy liquid on a desk near the entrance and set it back down, looking around uncomfortably. "You may have whatever you wish to take from your father's dormitory when you leave. I only ask that you leave the books as the majority belong to the library. Your timing is impeccable. Tonight is the celebration in the main dining hall in honor of your father."

Quistix offered a weak smile. "I'd like to attend that, if possible."

"I'll have it arranged. We will see you at dusk for the feast." The Headmaster stopped in the doorway. "Reach out if you need anything, Ms. Daetumal. It's been wonderful to see you again."

With that, she gently closed the door.

Eyes wide with wonder, Quistix moved toward a tiny kitchenette in the middle, complete with a countertop and cupboards. Near it sat a small, square dining table stacked with books and stray papers. A shiny metal trinket glimmered between the clutter and a book labeled *'Healing the Impossible.'*

Quistix plucked the trinket out of the pile. It made a metallic tinkling sound as she shifted it. Two small, pellet-filled balls were attached to a thin bar. It was a toy for a baby. A *rattle*. Small words had been carved into the metal along the bar that read:

My baby, you will always be.

Tears welled in her eyes. It was from the song she used to sing to Danson. She thought she had made up the words and melody, but holding the toy in her hands – *her* toy – she vaguely recalled her mother's voice singing it. She carried it through the room, gripping it tightly like a memory she didn't want to dissipate.

Twitch nudged her with an elbow and pointed to a large painting hanging on the wall of banners. It was of a man, woman, and baby. The woman had tangerine eyes and wild, copper-colored hair. She looked just like Quistix, only older.

The man was Eldrin, his green eyes in sharp contrast to his shock of red hair. His smooth-shaven face put him somewhere near his early 30s. The baby's citrine eyes were nearly identical to the mother's. The silver rattle hung out from the plump baby's mouth, held by chubby arms. A plaque affixed to the bottom read: *The Daetumal Family*.

"All this time, I thought he didn't care. I thought he discarded me. He sent me to live with my grandfather when I was five. Never visited. Never wrote. Why would he keep all of this?" Quistix anxiously rubbed her fingers against the etched rattle in her hand.

Twitch shrugged and moved onward. Near the one solemn window looking outside, at the end of the long stretch of room, sat a large straw bed with a beautifully carved tiaga headboard against the back wall, a nightstand on each side. An armoire sat nearby. Through its cracks, Quistix saw an array of thick robes with ornate designs around the flowery wrists of each.

"This looks like *Heaven* after where we've been sleeping lately!" Twitch sprawled out on the bed, snuggling the pillow, eyes pinched in ecstasy.

21

*Eldrin Daetumal's Dormitory Suite,
Institute of Magic, Apex City,
Apex*

The witch slept face-down across the bed, enjoying every available foot. Quistix sat at her father's desk, reading in the dim bloom of daylight. Her thoughts swirled. Several concepts in her father's tome surpassed her understanding. She found herself often distracted by his precise handwriting. Each swirl and dip in the letters seemed calculated and meticulous.

Day 192.

Today's revival testing was unsuccessful due to distractions. I lacked focus due to the Illuminator. *I have still not found yesterday's test subject. The*

Headmaster informed me that the green-eyed symph I'd been working with was spotted fluttering about the tower.

While it is reassuring for revival magic to show such promise during experimentation, I fear I'm approaching the boundaries of black magic. I may have to send away the Illuminator *for safekeeping. My ultimate goal is spell-creation, which any healer may use on the dead. Sadly, I feel my objectivity slipping as the trial progresses.*

I need *this to work. It* has *to work.*

There was a knock at the door. Twitch rolled onto his side, still asleep, groggily shouting, "Tell him I'm not here!"

A slender, elven man stood outside, poised to knock again as Quistix swung it wide open. She studied his gracefully aging features. A long, blond braid of hair laid against his left shoulder, draped below a formal hat. He clasped a wooden staff with a delicate, whittled bird perched on top.

"Good evening, I'm Cedrick, the ambassador." He reminded her of a skittish cat. "You and your wyl companion are formally invited to the dinner in your father's honor. Please head up to the formal dining hall." Without another word, he left.

Twitch pushed himself up on the bed, the fur around his mouth matted with drool. "Thank the Gods! I'm famished. We haven't had a proper meal since Samael's house."

Quistix's expression turned sour at the words. She felt horrible for repaying Samuel's generosity with outright robbery. She would find a way to repay him somehow.

22

*Vervaine's Quarters, Obsidian Palace,
Amethyst Cove,
Obsidia*

Vervaine dug through her vanity to find her mother's old hand mirror. Among the bevy of hairbrushes and pins, she found it. She grabbed the tarnished silver handle, angled the mirror toward her face, and was startled by the neon-green glow of her own eyes.

She gently touched the soft skin below, pulling down the lid to examine the eye. Beneath the lower lid were spidering gray veins throughout the whites. Her gaze moved down.

Her lips were void of vibrancy. Colorless and gray.

She wasn't herself anymore. She was trapped within her own body, every movement slow, as if paddling through an upstream river of thick molasses.

She touched the scarred side of her face, no longer shaken by the sight of it.

No longer shaken by the sight of *anything*, really.

23

Formal Dining Hall, Institute of Magic,
Apex City,
Apex

Everyone in the dining hall congregated in small cliques, milling and chatting as they found their seats. Brimming wine glasses dappled a long, thin table that could seat twenty or so. Candelabras made of clustered, magical orbs glowed orange along the center, illuminating fine crystal and imperial-looking dishware.

Madam Aerendyl waved for Quistix to sit beside her, then loudly addressed the gaggle of meandering wizards. "Thank you all for coming."

As they scooted their seats in, Twitch occupied the one across from Quistix, toasting her with his goblet from afar. A few chairs down, Professor Patteryl glared at the wyl in disgust, disgust, uneasily taking a seat.

"As you all know, this dinner honors our late alumni and professor, Eldrin Daetumal. We will serve some of Eldrin's favorite foods and share some kind words. We have a guest of honor this evening. His daughter Quistix is here." She motioned beside her and then clapped her hands together. "Now, who would like to start?

Professor Patteryl had a slicked-back head of earthy brown hair sprinkled with shimmering strands of white. His freshly-shaven face was oddly youthful and annoyed. "Professor Patteryl. I've been a librarian here for sixteen years. Never, in all that time, have I eaten with a wyl. This is an insult to all others who have graced this table. We are a school of superior learning, not a farm. If I wanted to dine with animals, I'd sit in a *pigpen*."

Quistix stood, grinding her molars in anger, but Twitch motioned for her to sit. As she did, he came around to her side of the table. "This night isn't about me. This is about your father. I refuse to tarnish that. I'll wait outside." He leaned in and pressed his furry snout to her cheek. He whispered in her pointed ear, "Just make sure you bring me some food. I'm *starving*." He smiled softly and walked out the door.

Professor Patteryl huffed and dropped to his seat.

The woman to his left stood, smoothing her sapphire robe. "I'm Professor Glenshire. Eldrin and I co-taught *Healing Magic* together. I also teach *Conjuration*. Before that, I was Eldrin's student. He taught me everything I know about the art of remedy. If I worked the rest of my days, I would never meet another like Professor Daetumal." She tucked a strand of honey-blonde hair behind her ear and returned to her seat.

The hefty man next to her arose, wiping his hands nervously on his violet gown. "Professor Opid, *Apothecary Sciences*. I've worked here for the past month as a substitute for Professor Daetumal." He looked at Quistix. "Sadly, I never met your father, but the students and the faculty all speak highly of him."

As he sat, another man in his 50s with a trimmed, graying mustache stood. "I'm Professor Teryl, and I teach," he stopped, "would you mind if I just *show her*, Headmaster?"

"Oh, you always *did* have such a flair for the dramatics," Glenshire mused, slapping him lightly on the leg with her napkin.

The Headmaster nodded, and Teryl stepped away from the table. He drew a circle around himself with the toe of his boot. From his palms, tendrils of blue smoke oozed out, pooling into a heavy cloud. He closed his eyes, inhaled, and threw his palms up. The cloud jerked and morphed, shape-shifting into an older man's face, its eyes stunningly familiar...

It was the face of Eldrin.

"I knew your father well. We graduated together. Eldrin Daetumal was brilliant." His breath hitched, and his eyes filled, ready to shed a tear over his deceased friend. "I conjure him occasionally to help me when I need inspiration."

Quistix struggled to focus on his words, absentmindedly nodding as she gawked at her father's image. The entrance door pushed open, and three large carts full of different entrees and sides flooded in.

"Ahh, the feast!" The Headmaster exclaimed, and the attendees rustled in their seats, prepping napkins and silverware at their settings.

An enormous bowl of mashed potatoes was rolled in first. Next, bowls of fresh salad and buttered asparagus followed by carts full of stuffed rabbits and sizzling noubald steaks. A large cart of sweet rolls and cakes burst through the doors.

Madam Aerendyl smiled. "Let's enjoy this meal in your father's honor while it's hot."

Quistix nodded, struggling to pull her gaze from her father's face in the conjured cloud.

24

*Amethyst Cavern,
Amethyst Cove,
Obsidia*

"I would like a progress report on *the Illuminator*." Exos held her chin down, shielding her day-glo green eyes below the wide brim of her hat. "Arias?"

Arias stood. "Your majesty, I tracked her up the Strogsend River, past Tamber Falls to Raven Cairn, where some accounts say she's still traveling with an esteg and a wyl. Word in Evolt is that they are headed toward the Platinum Cape, but no one seems to know why." Arias clasped his hands on the tabletop, staring down at them in shame.

"Alright. That's… something. Nictis?"

Despite her calm tone, the flaps of skin on her head stood half-erect.

"Nothing new to report, my queen. Just rumors and dead ends so far."

"Yet again, you are a worthless piece of semdrog filth. You're fired, Nictis. Your replacement, effective immediately, is Ceosteol."

Arias gasped, caught off-guard. The neon-eyed quichyrd stepped into the torchlight.

"Ceosteol? You cannot be serious! She's a traitor! Why isn't that old fool locked up?!" Arias slammed his fists down onto the tabletop.

"Ceosteol is no longer at large. I've given her a full pardon. She's been cleared of all charges. The guards of each state should have already received their notification letters."

Nictis scowled. "I'm being displaced by a murderous quichyrd with no experience training these animals?"

With a whirl of her talons, the growling infernal chained to the wall sat down, awaiting Ceosteol's next move.

"Ad illam exspecta me imperio." The infernal launched into a dead run, clotheslined by the chain on its leash, in an attempt to attack the semdrog. The quichyrd pulled back on the chains, unhooking it from its spot on the wall, and released the infernal. It raced forward, chains dragging, leaped onto the meeting table, and snapped at Nictis's face, stopping millimeters before her flesh. Green-tinted drool dripped from holes in its lips. Ceosteol held the chain tightly in her taloned fingers. The creature's snake-tail hissed.

"Promptus pro occiditis."

"You may control them, but they won't hurt me. They *know* me. I've spent a year training them! They don't bite the hand that feeds!" Nictis barked.

"You can avoid what I consider a *wildly entertaining* death, but only if you accept my terms." Exos laughed, her large-brimmed hat shielding the others from her day-glo green eyes. "You can stay employed cleaning the infernal pits and serving Ceosteol in whatever she needs."

Nictis looked away from the infernal, despite its snarling, to look Exos in the eye. "I would rather die than serve that twisted bird."

Exos nodded at the quichyrd.

"*Occidere!*"

With the simple utterance from Ceosteol's beak, the infernal lunged at Nictis's throat, knocking her backward. As they landed, the wolf's teeth tore Nictis apart, shredding and tugging its previous master's skin with the hunger of an animal near the brink of starvation. Nictis gurgled as she bled out over the harsh texture of the gemstone floor.

Once Nictis stopped moving, Exos stepped over the growing pool of semdrog blood. She leaned over Arias, her raven-black hair brushing his horns.

"Your men will assist with anything she requires for her work. Is that understood? Or does the infernal also need to explain it to *you*?"

The infernal snarled, face and paws covered in blood, exposed stomach bulging beneath decaying skin.

Arias stifled a growl. "Whatever you need, your majesty. I'm here to serve."

25

*Eldrin Daetumal's Dormitory Suite,
Institute of Magic,
Apex City,
Apex*

Quistix lounged at her father's desk, pouring through his massive tome. Each page told of a day in his life, experiments that had gone both right and horribly wrong. Hand-drawn illustrations depicted various spell incantations. Detailed drawings showed various plants used for alchemy.

The book was his career, his *life*.

"How's the book? Learning anything yet," Twitch asked, gnawing the cartilage from a plate filled with rib bones, specks of food strewn throughout the fur on his face.

"It's like I'm meeting my father for the first time." Quistix's orange eyes never peeled away from the tome.

Aurora and Frok were asleep, Frok squashed beneath a hefty textbook she'd been holding for the esteg. Aurora was out cold, her contented face on top of it.

"I know nothing about magic, and that's all this book has been about so far. It's like I have to start from his lessons at the beginning so I can even understand it. It discusses harnessing powers… concentration tactics… magic rings."

"What if you asked to join the college for a bit? Learn the jargon."

"I could never afford it. Plus, Exos would find me for sure if I stayed put for that long."

"I'll get you the money."

"Be serious. That amount of gold won't be in anyone's purse."

26

*Bluffs of Amethyst Cove,
Obsidia*

Standing high over the Jade Sea, overlooking the abyss beyond, Vervaine blankly watched the tide shift. She stepped to the edge, her toes hanging over the side, above falling pebbles tumbling hundreds of feet to the rocky coast below. She no longer felt calmed by the salty smell of the ocean and the sound of waves lapping, as she once had been.

The awe-inspiring view no longer brought her joy.

Nothing did.

Instead, a storm raged inside of her.

Her soul felt weak.

Trapped within itself.

She was a hollow, scarred shell of the woman she once was.

The woman she was before she died.

Nothing felt right since her return. It was as though she shared space in her mind with a darkened force crowding her into a tiny corner of her brain.

She wished she could dive in, head first, and let the water fill her lungs. Once and for all.

Would it actually end her suffering?

Or would it simply make this undead existence worse, she wondered.

She willed herself to leap, to end it all for *good* this time.

Like octopus tentacles, the quichyrd's magic felt like it was strangling her from all directions within her own body. The necromancer was violating the mere *pittance* of free will she had left. Just as her sister had for the years before her death.

She was just a deer, hunted in the wilderness by an army of *savages*.

Halting her attempt to die again, *this time by her own choice*, the ethereal tentacles within Vervaine drew her from the edge, forcing her feet backward until they were firmly planted on solid ground. She understood without even hearing the words.

The quichyrd wasn't done with her yet.

A voice deep down inside Vervaine screamed, but the sound never traveled to her lips.

27

*The Institute of Magic,
Apex City,
Apex*

The last two weeks had been long and arduous. Twitch found himself frequenting a tavern on the west side of town where he had taken a lover. He'd been cryptic about it when prodded at their nightly dinners in Eldrin's dormitory. The cheeky wyl hadn't been around much since they'd arrived. While Quistix had to admit she missed his presence, she was relieved to finally enjoy some complete solitude.

During that time, Aurora found herself ravenous, immersed in an almost endless wealth of knowledge, studying as if she'd be tested on the material. Her insatiable thirst for education and understanding led to long nights of falling asleep in piles of propped-up books while Frok ate everything they could scrounge up for her from the student mess hall. Though she'd gained almost half her body weight since coming to Apex, the bubbly little bottomless pit was having the time of her life exploring the vibrant gardens full of strange, magical mutations on her nightly flights alongside the esteg.

Quistix spent countless hours studying her father's tome, often dissecting chapters and practicing the incantations with Aurora late at night while the others slept.

Despite the elf's lack of funds, Headmaster Aerendyl offered to let Quistix participate in some of the training classes in exchange for crafting enchantable items for the students. Rings, metallic wands, and weaponry were crafted with incredible care and skill. Each item's craftsmanship and incredible attention to detail amazed even the most seasoned conjurer and alchemist. Quistix relaxed, knowing their summoned creations could never compare to the artisanship of a master blacksmith who, like herself, was forged in flames.

***

"You aren't concentrating!" Professor Teryl shouted.

An explosion of fire collided with the invisible barrier on the institute's lawn, startling the young students walking past. The shock wave rippled through, bending the indigo-tinged bubble like a bouncing drop of mercury.

Quistix eyed the cloud of smoke dissipating into the sky above and growled.

"Yes, I am! What else do you want me to do? I made the circle with my foot. I envisioned water—"

"You must block everything out. You're *frustrated*, hence the fire. There is too much rage in you!"

"I'm doing my best!" Quistix tugged angrily at the robe-tie around her waist.

"Take a break." Professor Teryl sighed and sat on a nearby stone bench, waving at a gaggle of students as they made their way past. "Come! Sit."

"I'm sorry, professor. I'm struggling." Her irises blazed white.

"Your parents were two of the most powerful elves in Destoria. I'm sure they had trouble in the beginning as well." He laughed, a hearty chuckle deep from his belly. "Your father once told me, when he was healing a patient with a particularly prickly personality, that he accidentally sealed the man's mouth. Thankfully, reopening it was a simple procedure, but your father was mortified." Teryl chuckled, and then his face grew somber. "Your father loved you deeply. He talked about you all the time. I felt like I already knew you when I met you."

He was so in love with your mother. For crying out loud, he even tried to bring her b—" Professor Teryl stopped himself, waving Quistix away. "You know, I think that's enough for today. Rest up. We'll try to make a waterfall again tomorrow."

He left, and she leaned back into the bench, the sun baking her despite the filter of the boundary bubble. The humid air covered her mouth like a wet cloth. She couldn't breathe, suffocated not by the sweltering heat but more so by a rich history that hadn't included her.

28

*Eldrin's Dormitory Suite,
The Institute of Magic,
Apex City,
Apex*

As the morning sun emerged, Quistix studied Eldrin's tome in the high-backed chair near the bed, her feet crossed on the mattress near Twitch's dreaming face. The esteg and pleom were already at the library again. The esteg's voracious appetite for books seemed unquenchable. Frok's half-eaten wheel of aged cheese lay on the floor, the smell of which permeated the air with Parmesan.

Quistix thumbed the rough slivers of parchment near the binding, where pages had been aggressively ripped out of her father's book, and gazed out at the sunrise through the indigo-tinted bubble around the floating city. The sky offered a burst of fiery colors with no clouds impeding the perfect view.

Quistix had burning questions that required answers. She looked out over the manicured grounds toward the administration building, which had to be easily a mile away. If she started toward the entrance now, she could catch the Headmaster before her hectic schedule was in full swing.

29

*Student Library,
Institute of Magic,
Apex City,
Apex*

Day after day, Annabelle Kybcheck sat in the same seat at the library, reading books alphabetically by author, in utter silence. During her years with the institute, she'd only managed to reach the books of *Eileen Balky*, whose early works covered the history of Destoria- as told by several of the original ewanian settlers. It contained 20 volumes, all dense and mentally exhausting. She was especially frustrated when Aurora rocketed through every volume in a matter of a day and a half.

The sound of Aurora's antlers accidentally *clacking* against the old wooden bookshelves every day made her blood boil. Every time, she reassured herself that soon her shift would be over, and the esteg and pleom would be Patteryl's problem for the remainder of the day. She felt as though she counted down the moments.

This morning, Aurora was reading a book by Paetle, a later work, from the propped-up text between her current reading pile. As the dragonling turned to the next page, she released a long, noxious fart, both long and loud, and remained seemingly oblivious.

The echo reverberated across the walls and pounded Annabelle's ears like a mallet. Unable to contain her rage, she slammed her book closed, rose, and swiftly approached the pleom, alarming the esteg with her long, aggressive strides. Lifting her cherubic head at the sound, Frok rubbed her sleepy eyes.

"Out! I have had enough!" Annabelle hissed sharply. "This is a library, not a *latrine*! Take the books and read elsewhere!"

30

*Headmaster Aerendyl's Office,
The Institute of Magic,
Apex City,
Apex*

Madam Aerendyl opened the blinds in her spacious office as Quistix settled into her seat. Gold-swirled crown molding, deep emerald walls, and an eye-agate-stone floor gave the room an air of importance and reminded them of the school's historical past. A large wooden desk adorned with neatly organized piles of papers and books sat between them.

Quistix caught her breath. She had forgotten how far the walk was, down all the sets of stairs and across the sky bridge, just to get to the administration building. Her legs stung from the hurried exertion, and carrying the heavy tome hadn't made things easier.

"To what do I owe this pleasure, Ms. Daetumal?" Aerendyl's voice was melodic, sing-songy. An obvious morning person.

"Reading my father's book, I've come across some pages that were ripped out. I thought I might ask if you knew where they went."

The Headmaster dipped her head glumly, her tone changing. "Unfortunately, they were confiscated from a student and placed in one of the high-security library vaults with the other forbidden texts."

"I don't understand. Why did a student have them?"

"He," she hesitated for a long moment, "entered Eldrin's room without permission and took them. He nearly killed himself and several others with the contents of those pages."

"He just broke in and stole them?"

"He didn't exactly break in. He had a key."

"Why would he have a key?"

"He," the subject caused her increasing shame, "took it from my key ring."

"That sounds like breaking in to me."

"It wasn't like he stole the key right off me in class. He had access to it at home. Eldrin was his father."

Quistix leaned back for a moment, taking the elf's words in and trying to understand what exactly it all meant. Her eyes widened when it hit her. "That boy in the infirmary."

"Yes." Her head drooped, and she glanced at the gardens beyond the window. "He's my son… with Eldrin. Which would make him your–"

"Half-brother." Quistix was stunned, her eyes dazed at what she was hearing. Her father had a whole life without her.

"Don't be angry. I know this is all a shock to you, and I probably should have told you sooner."

"Don't be angry?! My father abandoned me at five and sent me to live and work for my grandfather. Never visited. Never wrote. And had a new child that he's around every day. And I'm just supposed to be fine with this?"

"It's complicated–"

"Well, *uncomplicate* it, then! This doesn't seem very complicated. Loser father dumps his daughter and starts over. The end. He's not some great guy worthy of celebration dinners. He's a selfish bastard!"

"Now stop! Careful of the way you speak about *my late husband*. I'm not going to stand here and let you talk about Eldrin that way. Show some respect for the dead, at the very least. He had his reasons. After all, I've done to try to help you–"

"And why *are* you helping me?" Quistix raised her eyebrow, a stubborn one that didn't match her coffee-dyed hair. "Hmm? Is it pity because maybe he tossed me aside like I was nothing to him?"

"No! It's not like that!" Madam Aerendyl was yelling now, pounding her fist on her tiaga wood desk. "He would never just discard you. He loved you! He was a good man. He was just–"

"Just what?" Quistix fumed, her eyes slowly shifting to white before the Headmaster's eyes.

"Sit. Let me explain. I'll tell you what I should have told you the day you came here."

Quistix sat back down in her chair, irises dimming, pointed ears twitching. She rubbed the tome's cover without thinking, nervously searching for something for her hands to do.

Madam Aerendyl took a deep breath and spoke. "Eldrin Daedumal was a peculiar boy with a fascination for all things healing, particularly obsessed with the preservation of life. He studied here for years, as did your mother. He loved her more than anything." Those words made her voice waver, verging on tears. "Eldrin spent every free, waking moment with you once you were born. And at night, after they'd put you to sleep, your father would research preservation and restoration magics in the library, unsatisfied with the level of knowledge they were teaching in his courses." She tapped a quill nervously on a piece of parchment and continued.

"Lura, your mother, got pregnant a second time."

Quistix's eyes were no longer white, staring in wonder like a child hearing a tale around a campfire, captivated.

"There was a complication during the delivery. The child, a boy, was born stillborn, and your mother went into a seizure." Madam Aerendyl wiped her eyes. "My apologies. Lura was a close friend of mine." She composed herself, cleared her throat, and sniffled. "After she passed, your father fell into a deep, deep depression. He didn't eat. He barely slept. He started to get this… this look in his eye. I can't even describe it. It was chilling."

Madam Aerendyl locked eyes with Quistix. "I convinced your father to send you away."

The words ripped through Quistix like a bolt of lightning. She felt gutted. Suddenly, she understood why she'd been granted access to such an expensive program:

Guilt.

"I see. So with my mother out of the way, you wanted a clean slate for your new happy little family."

"No!" Madam Aerendyl was shouting again, unable to control her sudden outbursts. "That's not it at all!" She thought for a long moment, trying to find the right words. She opened her mouth to speak and closed it. Finally, sound came out. "Your father... became a darker force after Lura and the baby passed. I came to his room in the student dormitory one day to bring him some food. To make sure he was eating. To make sure you *both* were. I heard you crying, wailing through the door. When I came in, I was... I had never seen anything like it in my life."

She stood and walked around the desk, sitting on it, nearly touching Quistix with her knee. The sunbeams from the window lit up her crisp, colorful robe and shimmered across her nervous hands, grappling with each other as she spoke.

"Quistix, he had exhumed your mother's and brother's corpses from the burial gardens. She was lying on the bed, naked, your brother cradled in her arm. Above, you stood tied to the headboard. Blood was trickling from your wrists down onto them. Eldrin had a ceremonial dagger in his hand. His eyes were rimmed red with dark circles from the lack of sleep, gaunt from days of not eating. He was chanting from an old, yellowed book bound in flesh." She stared at Quistix for a moment.

"It was a book of black magic. Where he found it, I still don't know to this day."

Quistix looked down at her hands, which were mimicking the Headmaster's - nervously fidgeting - and then back up at the elf's sincere, crimson eyes.

"I wrestled him for the dagger, and he tried to cut himself in the process. I finally got it away from him, your father weakened by the sleep and lack of sustenance. He cried the whole night, and in the morning, I recruited a few trustworthy friends to help place their bodies back in the cemetery. The school's illusionist cast a sleep spell on him. He slept for three days straight. When he awoke, he had no recollection of what had happened. When I explained it to him, he fell apart all over again. The guilt over what he did to you… He felt like a monster."

"I don't… I don't know what to say." Quistix ran a trembling hand through her dark curls and exhaled deeply.

"Eldrin believed that book contained a spell that would bring them both back from the dead. But whatever is brought back with black magic… it isn't the same. *Ever*. What returns is something much worse. Something let loose from the darkness." Her tone grew sadder still. "For months, he was a broken man. I'd come to check on him just to make sure he was still alive and to feed you. I convinced him to send you to his father's farm where you could live a normal life until he had grieved and found himself again, which he did, reluctantly. And a year later, when he had gotten through the worst of it and risen to the top of his classes again, he came back to get you. He stood at the edge of the property, watching you, he said. Your grandfather was teaching you to work with metal. He said you were the spitting image of Lura, just smaller. He couldn't bear it. He returned, said you were better off without him after what he'd done, and we never spoke of it again."

Quistix's eyes welled with tears. She recalled the portrait under burlap in his dorm and how she did, in fact, bear a striking resemblance to her mother, Lura.

"Your father redeemed himself, over time, with his work and studies in healing magic. He helped so many people, saved countless lives, and trained others to do the same." She took a deep breath and exhaled slowly. "Well, over a decade after Lura's passing, your father and I courted in secret. I was up for Headmaster, and he'd gotten a job as the professor of Healing Magics. About a year after that, I became pregnant, and we eventually had a son."

Quistix recalled the affection the elf had shown the young man the day she arrived. "The boy in the infirmary?"

"Yes. He landed himself there with the same madness. So desperate to see his father that he pilfered my key, ripped out all the pages where your father spoke of his experiences with the reincarnation spells, and nearly killed a few of his fellow students trying to resurrect Eldrin." The tears fell freely now from her elven face. "Grief is a horrible thing. I miss your father every day. And now I have to expel my own son from the institute Eldrin, and I helped build." She sniffled. "Eldrin made a lot of mistakes. But he never thought of you as one of them. In fact, he'd often talk to you in his sleep, holding entire conversations. He always longed to have you in his life. He just couldn't bear it."

The Headmaster wiped her face and headed back to her seat. "He would have wanted me to allow you into the program. He'd be damned furious if I turned you away at the door, knowing your magical lineage. So you're here, training, because of him."

Quistix nodded, unable to process everything she'd just heard fully. Aerendyl's words were tumbling around like an emotional jumble in her brain.

As the Headmaster slid Eldrin's tome closer to Quistix in an effort to conclude the meeting, she spoke again, her tone soft but her words cold. "Eldrin was an amazing father to our boy. He doesn't know about you, and, in an effort to protect his memory of Eldrin, I'd prefer it to stay that way. He has enough to worry about right now with expulsion looming."

31

*Professor Opid's Classroom,
Institute of Magic,
Apex City,
Apex*

"There are magical people in the world. There always have been, and hopefully always *will* be. Hundreds of years ago, people like you were revered as Gods. Worshiped. Poised as leaders of nations. People like you have single-handedly devoured powerful armies and disintegrated continents. You are the best and the worst thing that has happened to Destoria."

"Some cultures try to breed magical abilities out by diluting bloodlines and prohibiting mages from associating. Other cultures ban the act completely, labeling us witches and wizards. Destoria is one of the few isles where mages can exist out in the open. We grow our forces here through bloodline continuations and honing our skills. Breeding between magical families can produce more powerful mages. "

Opid tapped on Quistix's piece of parchment, scribbled with notes from a quill she took from her father's dorm. The old man smiled down at her before continuing his circular shuffle around the desks in the classroom.

"Take Quistix here. Her bloodline is pure. Though only a novice, she remains naturally gifted due to her father and mother both having been mages themselves. Some people have to study their whole lives to do what she can. But if you focus your power and you learn how to concentrate it, you could protect the Destoria, even all of Feradona…" His tone grew serious, not a hint of a smile left on his face.

"Or you can *destroy* it."

32

*Uvege's Metal Works,
Apex City,
Apex*

Walking in, Quistix felt oddly at home. The metallic smell of freshly worked steel and smoke filled her lungs, calming her after the agitating morning. A steel sword propped on a stone stood out. It appeared to be a lower-quality metal than what she used in her workshop. She examined the curve of the blade and eyed the shoddy hiltwork. She tapped the tip of the blade on the wooden floorboard and listened to its reverberation. The metal sang for only a moment before going silent again. She scoffed at the poor craftsmanship.

"A sword like that would probably be much too heavy for a woman."

Unsure where the voice was coming from, Quistix looked around her, spotting no one. "How about a nice dagger instead? Or a short sword?"

"Shouldn't be a problem for someone like me." There was a hardened edge to her voice. She hated it when people thought her a distressed damsel.

She was rugged. *Tough.*
Underestimated.

On a second-level balcony, she spotted the source of the voice. He had the face shape and skin of an iguana. Spikes ran along his back, flexing with his breaths. He wore black cotton pants, ash-covered from working at a forge. His amphibious eyes were big and bright.

Never having seen a baiya before, Quistix was nearly speechless. "I take it you're *Uvege*?"

Walking down, he laughed loudly, his face nearly splitting in two as his massive mouth parted, jaws only connected by a thin stretch of pink skin. "Uvege was my grandfather. I'm Thaxl."

"Well, *Thaxl*." Quistix flipped the hilt in her hand, pointing to a spot on the blade. "You're heating the metal too long before you quench it. What color is it when you pull it from the coals?"

"Blue," he said slowly.

Quistix hissed sharply at his admission. "Who taught you to forge?"

The spikes on the back of Thaxl's head stood erect. "My father, who learned from his father, who learned from his father–"

"Well, I hate to break it to you, but someone along the way got it wrong. It should be the color of straw when you pull it from the coals. And, it's best to quench in oil, but I'll bet you're using water."

Thaxl fell quiet. "How…?"

"I was a blacksmith back in Bellaneau. Quenching at the precise time in *oil* yields a stronger, more flexible weapon.

He tipped his head to the side, swallowing his pride. "Interesting." He flashed a bright smile. "Well, now that I know I'm in the presence of an expert, is there anything I can help you find? Anything you're looking for?"

"Just browsing." She turned her full attention to his shelves of weaponry and boxes of rings, necklaces, and hair clips below, all made of the same materials, some adorned with flawed gemstones.

"Great. Feel free to look around and ask questions." He wiped his claws on his apron and studied her. "You in that school a'magic?"

"Yeah… well, sort of." She sighed. "I guess not really. My time there is up soon. I'll be traveling back to the mainland on Woragor."

"Well, I dunno what that means, but you look like the *type*. We don't get many elves in here that aren't students or faculty. Hell, we don't get many elves in here at all. We mostly supply the staff, as a matter of fact."

"Yeah?" She said, half-listening and examining his other wares and various metal creations for any diamonds in the rough.

"You got any armor?" He sounded curious, on his tip-toes leaning over the counter to get a better view of what she was eyeing. "Good set 'a armor'll go a long way on your travels. There's a lot of stuff out there that wants to kill an elf like you."

She laughed. "I'm well aware."

"So…?" He was waiting for her to actually answer his question.

"I used to." She recalled the flames licking her home in Bellaneau nearly a year ago. "Why? You got some in a back room or something? All I see up here are weapons and jewelry."

"Well, if you ever do need some, keep in mind you need pieces fortified to withstand your abilities. I saw one of those kids cast a fire spell outside of the college one night," He whistled, "fused the breastplate right to his skin! Turned the metal molten in seconds. He died. *Painfully*."

That caught her attention. She remembered her clothes turning to ash in the Emerald Bandit's Den when her eyes blazed white. "So, does someone make a special kind of armor for our kind?"

"Yeah, but magic-compatible ain't common. Even 'round these parts."

Her shoulders slumped. He weaved through some display shelves and leaned in close, then looked around to make absolutely sure they were alone.

"I know where you can find some, though. If you buy something here today, I'll tell you where to find it. It's not a far walk from here."

She laughed. "Now you're just pullin' my leg."

"No! Swear on my wife's unborn eggs! It's a breathtaking set, I've heard." He looked genuine. "Just… think about the offer. I have a few magical items up front, including a locket for focus that someone just traded in."

She snickered. "How much is the locket?"

"Fifty gold."

She giggled and started to exit the shop. His reptilian hand shot into the air, fingers splayed.

"Wait! Twenty gold."

"Ten and directions. Final offer."

He thought for a moment and then nodded. "Fine." He held out his hands. She fished a handful of coins out of her satchel. She barely had enough to cover the cost.

"I guarantee you. It'll be the best ten gold you ever spent."

"If it's not there, I'm coming *back*." She locked her citrine eyes on his. Her threat was vague, but the message got through.

"You're going to be amazed when you see it. I've heard rumors that it's pretty legendary. And it's the whole matching set, too. All magic-fortified. It'll be perfect for you. I just saved you a whole heap a' money!"

"We'll see about that."

He retrieved the focus locket and gently laid it in her hand. He leaned over the counter. "Okay. So this old witch was buried in it out at the Greatwich Tombs outside'a the city. Problem is, it's in her tomb."

"Great." She scoffed. "I'm raiding a casket?"

"Pfft, shouldn't be any problem for someone like you, right?" He said, echoing her own words back to her. "It's the biggest tomb in the cemetery; you can't miss it."

33

Level of Conjuration,
Institute of Magic,
Apex City,
Apex

"Picture a creature and its motivation. You're creating a temporary new life with its own driving force. If you are unfocused or frustrated, the more likely you are to create a being that will harm yourself or other innocents." Professor Glenshire tapped her wrists, nudging them into the air.

"Alright, alright." Quistix rubbed her necklace of focus and relaxed her shoulders. She held out her hand, fingers splayed.

Her eyes glowed.

Before her, from the ether, Samael appeared. The angry barbarian who'd taken them in Raven Cairn stomped toward her, his face full of rage over the violation of his trust. The guilt was still fresh in her mind. They repaid his kindness with burglary. She felt shame as she looked into his furious eyes, tucked beneath a furrowed brow.

As he neared her, rearing his enormous fist to assault her, his conjured image faded into dust.

Quistix collapsed, drained, and crumpled into the circle on the floor, panting hard.

"Fantastic work!" Professor Glenshire clapped her gloved hands together and smiled, her cheekbones raised high.

"That's exhausting." A smile spread on Quistix's face as she clambered to her feet. "But... I think I did it!"

"You did! Rest up. I'm going to make you do it again. Next time, for longer. And remember," she manipulated the elf's hand, posing it differently than before, "the most concentrated magic comes from your palm. Your fingers are only for intricate magic that requires more specific guidance." Glenshire smiled. "Magic is as unique as the caster. It is as pure as your intentions and as strong as your will. Your father was amazing, and your mother, dare I say, was even better than he. I know this is your last day, and I'd be remiss if I didn't say that you've got something very special in you. Keep practicing. I firmly believe if you *do*, and do so *often*, you will become a legendary mage, up there with greats like Hadina and Merlin."

34

Eldrin's Dormitory Suite,
Institute of Magic,
Apex City,
Apex

The weeks had blown by, and Quistix found herself in her father's long chamber, surrounded by his passions and creations getting ready to leave it, possibly for good. Though he'd sent her away at a young age, she felt as if being in his space taught her things about him, most importantly, that he didn't forget about her all those years ago. She'd found trinkets from her childhood sparking vague memories of their brief and formative time together, along with a stash of letters to her that he'd written but never sent. She'd spent hours poring over them, night after night, once the others had gone to sleep. They felt like a conversation she'd longed to have for so many years, even if one-sided.

Now, glumly, she shuffled about the skinny room, sifting through items and packing a small bag full of important things. Though she had no home to display them, keeping them near felt like having a piece of Eldrin close by. She wanted the painting most of all as it's the only thing that kept her parent's faces vivid in her memory. But with no home, it had to be abandoned. After all, it would never make the dragon ride back to Destoria, something she was both thrilled and terrified to do again.

As she examined the painting one last time, she thought about the irony. Once, she had felt discarded by them. Now, she was in the same position.

A knock at the door tore her from her thoughts.

She thought it might be Twitch and Aurora, anxious to leave Apex despite her offer to meet them on the sky bridge shortly to save them the trek.

But when she opened the door, she was greeted, instead, by Headmaster Aerendyl's warm, elven smile and bright ruby eyes.

"Pardon, Quistix, but I wanted to catch you before you left. I wanted to say goodbye, and I also have a gift." She fidgeted nervously with her hands as Quistix welcomed her inside. "I see you aren't taking much."

"I have to travel light and, unfortunately, I don't have a place to call my own at the moment.

I'd have loved to have taken some of these things. Your son is welcome to take the rest."

The words sounded so strange. *Your son. I mean, my brother.*

"That's kind of you. I'm sure that will mean the world to him. He misses Eldrin so much. We all do. His loss leaves a hole in all of us." She sounded solemn. "Make sure you take Eldrin's tome if you want. Tome's are personal property here."

"Thank you."

"You have an incredible gift. Don't squander it." She anxiously jingled the item in her hand. "Oh, I had the opportunity to speak with Aurora on a few occasions, and I have decided to integrate an interspecies training program and offer scholarships next semester. Please let her know she would be welcome to apply. Students have full access to the library, and we could certainly use a healer like her in our infirmary ward."

"I'll let her know. She'll be excited to hear that." Quistix forced a smile despite the melancholic circumstances.

The Headmaster held out a coin purse. "Your professors and I took up a collection to cover your flight back with Veynan. It should be enough."

Quistix was speechless. She wasn't about to tell the Headmaster that Twitch had pick-pocketed enough to cover the fee and a night at the inn near the landing spot in Evolt. Or that he'd pilfered enough food from the mess hall to feed them all for several days.

"And hearing about your unfortunate circumstances with the fire–"

"Who told you about that?" Quistix didn't even let her finish.

"Well, Twitch mentioned it. He said you lost nearly everything due to a bandit raid."

She wasn't surprised the wyl blabbed. She just shook her head and stared at the floor.

"I know Eldrin didn't know that I knew about this," she walked to the ceiling-high bookcase, glanced at several titles, and then plucked one nearly out of reach. She handed it to Quistix. "This one doesn't belong to the library. You should keep it. Use it toward a fresh start."

Quistix laughed at the title, reading it aloud, "Financial Success for Mages?"

She flipped the book over to look at the back and heard metal jingling inside. With an eyebrow raised, she opened the front cover, revealing the contents had been hollowed out with a knife. In the carved-out nook sat a fistful of platinum pieces. Her tangerine eyes enlarged.

"I don't think I can take this." She offered the book to Aerendyl and thought about how Twitch would curl into a ball and die if he saw her attempting to turn away that much coin.

Aerendyl pushed it back at her gently. "I insist. Eldrin would have wanted you to have it."

"I don't know what to say." The voice caught in her throat.

"Say goodbye." The Headmaster smiled. There were tears in her eyes. She hugged Quistix hard and primped the warrior's coffee-dyed hair after she pulled away. "Safe travels, Quistix. I wish you the best of luck."

35

*The Skies Above Evolt,
Evolt*

The ride back to Evolt was brisk and exciting. At the request of Frok, Veynan had taken them all for a loop, quite literally. For a moment, the distracted elf thought they might all plummet into the foaming green-blue waters of the Jade Sea below. Exciting tricks seemed to bring the ancient creature great joy. Instead of soaking in the surroundings, Quistix thought about the spells she'd learned at the Institute of Magic, a deep feeling of unexplained dread rising in her stomach regarding her future. She had no idea where to go or what might lie ahead. She had no home or place to lay her head. No child. No parents.

Just a cryptic book full of resurrection nonsense written by her dead father, a few basic spells she could practice, a book full of money, and an outfit of her mother's she'd taken from the drawer at the base of her father's armoire.

And she had her friends. That thought made her smile as she looked out over the rag-tag group of misfit tag-a-longs she'd amassed in her journey for retribution and knowledge, all three clinging to Veynan, the now cobalt-blue dragon, with wind-manipulated grins on their faces. They seemed to be having the times of their lives, soaring high above Destoria, eyeing a view most would never be lucky enough to see *once*, much less *twice*, in one lifetime.

As Veynan touched its taloned feet into the crunching snow below them, Quistix felt more lost than ever. They had to make one very out-of-the-way stop, but after that, she had no idea how to stop the Destorian army from hunting her or where she should go next. Maybe she'd start over on the sister isle where no one knew her. Perhaps, start anew.

After all, they say Asera is nice this time of year, she thought.

36

Samael's Home,
Outskirts of Raven Cairn,
Evolt

After several weeks away, she couldn't believe the dogsled had still been there when Veynan touched down near the Lush Beaver Inn. She thought it a stroke of luck, though the massive creature assured her that the goblin-toll worker prided himself on the safety of his rider's possessions. The owner of the Lush Beaver even allowed him to rent a storage shed behind the inn for such things. They'd said their goodbyes, strapped the reins onto Aurora, and she mushed them all north, through the snow, back to the outskirts of Raven Cairn and the familiar humble shack where the smell of bubbling stew seethed from the smoky fireplace.

Ever since they'd left, Twitch's burglary gnawed at her conscience. She rapped on the door and flinched when it opened, preparing for a potential assault.

It was Samael. His face contorted in a frown when he recognized her and Twitch, both red-nosed, standing in the doorway. He started to close the door on her when Twitch pressed on it gently, forcing it to stay open.

"Please, hear us out." His wyl voice was small, like a pup. "I'm sorry, Samael. You took us in. You fed us. Bathed us. You gave us a sled. I was wrong to take from you. We were in need of coin, and I thought," his words dripped with remorse, "You're a good man. You didn't deserve what I did to you. For a long, long time, I was a member of the Thieves Guild and stealing became a second nature."

"We came back to try to make it right," Quistix said, extending a small, bursting coin purse.

Samael took it with hesitance, peering into the bag as if it contained something that might bite. "This is too much. You only took four–"

"There's extra as reparation. We wronged you, Samael. And I'm truly sorry." Quistix stared at the floorboards, her breath fogging the air between them in gray, billowed puffs.

A soft smile spread across Samael's face. "Would you like to come in? Wife's got stew on. She always makes plenty. Just keep your sticky fingers to yourself this time. Do it again, and we'll be having *Wyl* stew next."

***

It felt good to get out of the frozen tundra and warm their feet by the fire. The stew was rich and full of vegetables from their well-stocked root cellar.

"So what was it like inside? I've heard it's massive!" Samael's wife asked, leaning forward with excitement.

Samael waved Quistix into his daughter's room, and she slipped away, unnoticed.

"The institute is sprawling! There's this massive bridge that takes you from the entrance to the actual tower with the school and dormitories, which, in itself, is an exhaustively huge piece of property. The main tower," Twitch carried on, sparing no detail about their adventures in Apex.

In Hilde's room, Samael reached into his thick cotton flannel and produced a rolled piece of parchment with a torn shred of fabric around it.

On the side of the roll, it read *Quistix* in cursive handwriting.

"What's this?" She asked, standing nearly toe-to-toe with the hulking barbarian in the tight quarters. "Whatever it is, I can't take it. You've already done so much."

"It's not from me. A few hours after you left, I found a carrier wolf scratching at the front door, trying to get in. He had this tied to his neck. He musta smelled your scent here. Those wolves they got a sniffer on them that is damn near magical. I thought about sending it to Apex with a symph, but after I realized the money was gone, I didn't think you deserved the courtesy. I couldn't throw it out, either. Just didn't seem right." He looked apologetic, offering it to her. As she took it, he smiled and patted her hand closed around it with his own, both nearly double the size of her own mitts. With that, he left, boots clunking down the wooden hallway planks back into the main room.

She untied the sash and unfurled the letter, already knowing who it was likely from... *Kaem.*

It read:

Quistix,

Old friend, I hope this finds you well. I hate to ask this of you, but Ralmeath and I could use your help. We received a new mission after we saw you. We were hired by Queen Exos to poke around about some missing money and Biagio berries that went missing. Without them, the main dikeeka supply will soon halt. But ever since we got to Desdemona, it's clear that Exos hasn't been acting right, nor has Vervaine. On top of that, do you recall Ceosteol? The old quichyrd who did all of those horrible tests on wyl children all those years ago? She's still alive and has received a full pardon, which doesn't make sense considering the old quichyrd's crimes. She's not only been freed but seems to have become close to royalty. Too close. *I've had some interesting chats with those closest to her, including the new head of the royal guard, Arias, and her flaming bandit lackey, Omen.*

We are going to poke around some more, but I sense danger brewing. I've heard multiple rumors of undead creations spotted roaming near the Palace. Something isn't right. I could really use your help, Lux Alba. I would have never asked, but since the bounty has been removed from your head, I thought you could use some adventure. There's gold in it for you, too.

Ralmeath and I will be just west of Desdemona out at the old Newberry Ranch, and we hope you will join us there as soon as you're able.

If you're coming, please hurry.

With honor,

–Kaem

Quistix wondered if it was a trap to lure her right to Exos for reward money. *No,* she thought. *That couldn't be it. If Kaem were trying to lure her, she would have done it in a much cleverer way.* Kaem was anything but obvious. Plus, after knowing the quichyrd for decades, she couldn't imagine a world where Kaem would be that heartless.

***

After speaking with Twitch and Aurora, the consensus was that they were all ready for an exciting new caper.

"Why did she say the bounty has been removed?" Twitch looked just as puzzled as Quistix was.

Samael giggled as he threw another frozen log on the fireplace. The iced firewood hissed as the raging flame melted it. "They took your bounty signs down in the bar weeks ago. Must have been a day or two after you left for Apex. When I asked if they were replacing them with newer sketches, the guard said no. Said they were no longer searching for you. I assumed they must have intercepted you before you boarded Veynan."

"Any idea how we could get to Desdemona quickly? Think Veynan would take us?"

"Veynan would charge an arm and a leg for that trip if you even got the goblin to agree. Some of my buddies from the tavern where I met you were headed to Outliar's Docks to haul the last few crates of dikeeka over that way. I could see what I could do about getting you on that boat. He owes me a favor, so I think I can get him to take you. But we would need to hurry. I don't know when they're set to leave, but I know it's soon."

37

*Outliar's Docks,
The Jade Sea,
Evolt*

A large wooden ship sat stoically at the edge of the dock offering transport into the unknown. Sheets of ice littered the water's surface, bobbing in the tumultuous white-capping waves.

The captain adjusted the tie on his black, woolen overcoat soaked with the stench of sea salt and body odor. Stringy hair flapped about his head in the chilled breeze, caked with oil and dirt. His eyes were red-rimmed with exhaustion, stomach growling from a lack of food.

As Quistix and her comrades said their goodbyes to Samael, the captain flashed his barbarian pal a toothy grin, one filled with yellowed teeth and receding gums.

"I'll take good care of 'em for ya'," he chortled.

Quistix and Twitch smiled politely and seated themselves on large crates marked DIKEEKA across from a tight-lipped ewanian bundled in his calf-length noubald coat. The crate reminded Quistix of her late husband's indiscretions, ones that led to his eventual demise. The sight of the painted words made her feel colder than the frosty air.

Aurora gazed out over the water, deep in thought. The sporadic wind gusts ruffled through her fur. The dragonling slept swaddled in a rabbit pelt within the hammock, protecting her scaly skin from the breeze.

And with the unwinding and tossing of a solitary, frayed rope, they were off, traveling through the narrows of Platinum Cape northbound at a surprisingly brisk pace.

***

The boat had clearly seen better days. The fog was thick, and the wind was punishing. On the first night of their voyage, the watercraft rounded the corner at Glacier Strait. Quistix didn't know she could be this cold and live. Even on the coldest days on their secluded butte in Bellaneau, it hadn't seemed nearly as cold as it did on the Jade Sea. Quistix and Twitch huddled for warmth, their fur coats vibrating with their shivers.

As they passed the prison, the ewanian shipmate tapped the captain, waking him from his slumber. They switched places, the captain back at the helm, and the ewanian slid a pry bar out of his tool kit and used it to open a crate.

The captain flashed him a sideways glance as if to mildly chastise the behavior. Still, the ewanian just smiled and said, "Aww, c'mon. They ain't gonna miss one little bottle."

With that, he removed a vial of black liquid, closing the crate with his slick green fingers around the top of the bottle. With a squeeze, he broke apart the red wax seal over the top of the cork and yanked it loose. He held the vial up towards Quistix. "Ladies first?" It sounded more like a question than an offer.

She shook a hand at him, making a sour face. "I don't partake. That stuff made me a widow."

"How's 'at?" He asked, tossing a swig back with abandon.

"Long story." She blew fog from her lips as she exhaled. He shrugged and looked around. "I got time. Nothing *but*, actually."

"Well," she paused, unsure why she was sharing something like this with a complete stranger. She didn't even know his name. Though, she figured he might be affected by a cautionary tale. "My husband, Roland, was a city guard in Vrisca. Excelled at his job. One day, he caught a young barbarian stealing bread from the market. He tried to stop the kid to give him a talking-to but was met with a knife instead. The boy stabbed him in the side three times. Nearly died from the infection. Nothing seemed to stop the pain. I wish I'd known an esteg at that time." She laughed lightly and looked up at the starry night sky, triplet moons shining bright.

"One day, another guard visited him in the infirmary. He offered him dikeeka that he'd confiscated from a dealer. He was going to turn it in but offered it to Roland instead. He took it. Made a miraculous recovery but became sick in a different way. He made it his mission to always get more and more. He told himself he was just doing his job, cleaning up the streets, even if it was going down his own gullet. He gained a temper that he never had before. He grew moody and would turn on my son and me in a moment. Had this gaunt look about him, always smelling of sickly-sweet sweat and biagio berries. Every day, it snuffed a little more of the light out of him. In the end, before it took his life, he was a shell of the man I married."

The ewanian looked at the rest of the bottle suspiciously and corked it, pocketing the remnants for later.

"It was tough at the end, watching him waste away, but I still miss who he was before that damn curse-in-a-vial." She wiped the dampness from her eyelashes to keep it from turning to ice. "Every day."

A hushed solemness fell over them all as the vessel rushed onward, water churning wildly below. The cloudy haze on land thinned, revealing a silhouetted landscape with Strogsend Brig perched on the hillside. Its battered clay walls were surrounded by whipped piles of snow, like white desert dunes.

***

"Starlight Lake is back 'at way, about a half-a-day walk from the shore." The captain said to Twitch, grateful to have company at the helm.

Aurora's ears perked up. "That's where we're from!"

Frok popped her head out of the hammock, her face plastered with a look of pure excitement. "That means we's close to Glitter Gulf!"

"Ayuh, we're actually in it right about now. Gotta go right through it to get to Desdemona. It's not yet the season for the glimmer fish to school. Most are still out in the deeper waters, but if you look over the side, who knows. You might get lucky."

Frok fluttered her portly body to the side of the wildly rocking boat and peered into the water, her little head staring with its comically wide sapphire eyes into the white-capped waters.

"Careful being that close to the edge, Frok. I don't want you to fall in." Aurora mothered.

"I won't! Jeez, 'Rora!"

"She's right, I wouldn't get too close–" The ewanian's words were cut short. Before he could finish his thought, the boat rocked, and Frok tumbled in.

The splash was like a thrown cannonball blasting the churning surface.

"Frok!" Aurora screamed, her hooves clattering around the wooden floorboards in a scramble.

Quistix stood, whipped off her coat, and prepared to dive. Twitch held her back. "Are you kidding? Q, that water's freezing. That's suicide." He looked at the ewanian, terror in his eyes. "Do you have a rope or something we can throw down for her?"

"He's gonna eat her!" The captain said, shaking his head, hands firmly on the wheel. The passengers seemed confused by what he meant. Everyone except the ewanian.

"Get her out," the amphibian hollered, "there's a *grindylow* down there!"

"I thought those were made up!" Quistix shouted.

"What do you think's been powering the *boat*?!" The captain chuckled, his gaze locked on the water in front of him. Suddenly, the boat's forward motion halted completely as if they'd been anchored into place.

The ewanian watched nervously, his throat-sac pulsing.

Beneath the frozen waves, Frok's bulbous body tensed. She fluttered her huge eyes in the green-tinged murk and swam toward the surface. She could hear Twitch's muffled, frantic voice.

A shaded figure swam toward her from below the boat's bow, stopping it still in the water. Its movements were fluid and swift. He had the head of a vicious fish, with a long face and rows of gnashing teeth - like a muskie. Eyes blinking oddly like an alligator. He bore the pale body of a thin human with webbed extremities, taut around the ribs and sunken in the stomach. Horns on the top of his head wound back like an ibex.

He snapped his fangs at her, nearly catching her plump foot in his maw. Frok was certain he could've eaten her whole if she'd been just a few inches closer.

Water rushed down her throat as she tried to scream.

An anchor splashed through the water beside her, and Frok swam to it, catching it just in time as

Twitch and Quistix dragged it back to the boat with all their might.

She held on with her tiny, clawed hand, clenching her eyes shut tight. The pleom was yanked upward with the anchor. Inches from the boat's edge, the Grindylow thrashed, slapping at her with a webbed hand. She felt turtle-like claws at the end of each drag across her side. She opened her eyes to see blood in the water.

Her blood.

She opened her mouth and sucked in a lungful of iced seawater just before she broke the surface. She coughed violently, sputtering and gasping for chilled air as they pulled her aboard.

"I'm so glad you're alright!" Quistix examined the damage.

Frok began to cry. She was traumatized.

"It looks like the wounds are minor. Aurora?" Quistix had the worried look of a mother in her eyes.

Aurora looked at the wound, and with teary eyes, she bent forward and touched her glowing horn to the pleom. The horns glowed brighter on contact, and Frok's wounds soon healed. The ewanian and captain watched the exchange, utterly fascinated.

"I… I was so scared, 'Rora!"

The ewanian grabbed a baggie of rank fish parts and dumped it into the water at the front of the boat. The water churned like a piranha-feeding zone as the pieces were devoured.

Moments later, the boat lurched forward again, placing the vessel back en route.

"What were you thinking, Frok!" Aurora growled. She turned to Twitch, trying to mask her frustration and, more importantly, her fear. "Please, wrap her in your coat, or she'll catch her death."

Twitch bundled the pleom against the fur of his chest and hugged her tightly to share his body heat. Muffled words arose from his fur coat. He stared down. "I can't hear what you're saying."

His lapel flaps parted, and the dragonling's snout pressed out. Her tiny mouth cried, "I just wanted to see the glimmer fishies!"

38

*Newberry Ranch,
Outskirts of Desdemona,
Willowdale*

"By the Gods, Quistix, is it good to see you!" Without another thought about it, Kaem quickly spanned the frosted farmland between them. She wrapped her scarred arms and tattered wings around the elf in a loving cocoon of opalescent, black feathers and squeezed hard. "I thought for sure you weren't coming."

"It took me a while to get your correspondence. We went to Apex."

"Oh, you make friends with all the fuddy-duddy elves up there?"

Quistix scoffed a little. "It's a strange place, Apex."

"Never been. Heard a lot of stories, though. Seems like too snooty a place for a battle-torn quichyrd like me." She pulled back and ran her taloned fingers along the elf's espresso braid, the red beneath beginning to reappear. "Interesting new look."

"Damn reward posters were everywhere. The red was a dead giveaway."

Ralmeath erupted in a terrifying roar behind them. Kaem let the hair drop and looked back at the Bramolt bear, slowly following behind. She shushed her, turned back to Quistix, and chuckled. "Ral gets *jealous* sometimes."

"I see that." Quistix offered a wave to the bear as soon as Kaem released her.

Twitch waltzed up to Ralmeath, bowed a little, and took her enormous paw in his. He kissed the top of it like a proper gentleman. "So we meet again, beautiful. I never forget a gorgeous face."

Quistix laughed. The bear had to be at least four times his size. Yet, it squirmed bashfully at his flirtation.

"You remember Twitch from the last time we saw you, I'm sure. We met these two shortly after. The esteg is Aurora and the... well," She looked at the pleom whose sapphire eyes were peering up over the swath of fabric between Aurora's glowing horns. "You tell her." She winked.

Frok exploded out of the hammock with glee, straight into the air like a cannonball. "I's Frok! I's a pleom!"

"She loves a grand entrance." Quistix shook her head.

"So does Dally, our pleom... for now. He's a clumsy little fool. He's out in the pasture if you want to go meet him."

"A buddy? Can I?!" Frok's excitement was at its maximum limit. She sounded like she might explode from it. Kaem nodded, and Aurora followed the direction of the quichyrd's nod.

Kaem leaned toward Quistix and whispered, "liberated him and a few others from a blitzed reptilian a few days ago, and he just won't leave, so I've been giving him little tasks so he can feel like he's helping."

"They're great for starting campfires."

"Good to know." Kaem cocked a brow and smiled. "He eats more than Ralmeath. I don't know how much longer we can keep him."

"Frok's the same. How can something so small eat so much? I don't understand it."

Kaem pulled away from the elf and started toward the ranch house at the edge of the property, waving for them to follow. "I'd love to spend more time catching up, but I'm afraid we should get down to business right away. No time to waste."

Twitch and Quistix followed dutifully, with Ralmeath following at the rear. Quistix looked around, soaking in the rustic setting. She eyed the pens and field. All empty. Not an animal in sight.

Something was strange. She could feel it in the air.

A surge of nervousness ran through her spine like a cup of icy water. "Catch me up to speed, Kaem."

***

Aurora lay in a bed of hay beneath a gnarled oak with naked branches, watching the two excited pleoms chitter like old friends even though they'd just met. Dally was a light shade of forest green with emerald eyes that were nearly a third of the size of his dragonling head. Slightly bigger than Frok, he fluttered with a little more strain as they flitted around like fattened hummingbirds, laughing and getting to know each other.

Aurora was so glad to see her in such high spirits, especially after nearly losing the pleom to a hungry grindylow.

"We isn't owned! We is free creatures!"

"And 'den, what happened?" Frok's voice was full of childlike wonder.

"Then 'da bird lady took me in the cage, and once we was away from 'dat lizard, she made 'da bear smack 'da cage on a rock til I was free!"

Both pleoms fluttered to the low bough of the tree over Aurora. Their ecstatic voices echoed out over the vast expanse of ranchland.

"Wow, dat's amazing!"

"Where are you from?"

"I's from Starlight Lake!" Frok's skin blushed.

"Me too!" Dally exclaimed at maximum volume.

"No way!"

"Have you ever seen a raakaby?" The change in subject matter had no segue, and it didn't seem to bother either of them.

"Yes! It had colorful wings and long furry ears! But dey have venom too!"

"The one I saw had that too!" Frok's giant sapphire eyes were bulging now.

"You has nice eyes," Dally said with a bashful smile, his forest green coloring growing more intense.

Frok blushed more and twisted bashfully at the waist.

"There's a dwagon named Veynan 'dat takes you to Apex! He's blue, too!"

"No way!" Dally's voice made him seem as infantile as Frok. "Wow, you seen the whole world!"

"I guess I have!"

After a moment of unusual silence between them, Dally took her cheeks in his tiny, clawed hands and said, "You 'da purdiest thing I ever seen."

***

Night had set over the quaintly decorated farmhouse. By lantern light, everyone but Frok and Dally had gathered around the large donik table, reviewing a map of Willowdale. They savored the stove's heat as it blazed beside them, mightily combating the frigid night air that crept inside. Debating their plans, they remained seemingly oblivious to the man's terrified, faint screams in the distance.

"Ceosteol is *evil*, Q. During our investigation, Ralmeath and I discovered the old bird had amassed an army of these undead *playthings*. Ceosteol was recently formally pardoned by Exos, which is curious. She should have been *hanged* for her sickening crimes decades ago, but I guess due to some familial sympathy from the Tempests, she was imprisoned instead."

"What were her crimes?" Aurora questioned with hesitant curiosity.

"You haven't *heard*?" Kaem was awash with genuine surprise. "Some years ago, Ceosteol was caught in a shack in the woods here in the wilds of Willowdale. She was experimenting on wyl children, practicing her necromancy and blood magic spells, attempting – and succeeding – in making these twisted, sinister new creations. Sewing children together and sealing the seams with her potions. Combining parts, mixing species. Trying to make a superior species or something. So many wyls went missing that she switched to woodland creatures to keep from arousing too much suspicion. One of her favorites was a two-headed wolf with a snake for a tail. Called them *tailed infernals*."

"Yeah, we actually encountered one of those a few weeks back." Twitch piped up. "Thing was vicious and smelled *horrible*. Some guy with a flaming face had them on a leash. He came at Quistix. They fought, but then he sort of... *evaporated*."

Kaem frowned.

"What?" Quistix stepped toward her, alert.

"That's... Omen. He's one of our men on the inside. Used to be the head chief of the Emerald Bandits until Exos demoted him to the jailer at the Infernal Caverns, where the queen's sister, Vervaine, was being held for... no one really knows what for. Some conspiratorial paranoia–"

"Are you *kidding* me? I can't fight alongside him! He's a monster!"

"He's on our side, Q! He's been providing us with intel for weeks, drawing these maps. He wants these things annihilated as much as we do."

"That doesn't make any sense!"

"He's cursed by Ceosteol, Lux." Kaem sighed heavily. "Long story short, he got blamed for Exos trying to kill her sister, Vervaine, when they were just girls. King Tempest subsequently ordered him to be cursed to burn eternal by Ceosteol. It seems that, just like these other undead beings, his soul is tied to hers through black magic. From what I understand, if we destroy *her*, we simultaneously put everything she's soul-tied to out of its misery. Including *him*."

"The Emerald Bandits killed my son, Kaem. You can't possibly understand what you're asking of me when you want me to team up with him! Danson is gone. *Forever*."

"A lot of other mothers are going to be losing their children too if we don't stop this. If we don't wage war now, there'll soon be too many to fight. Plus, if we succeed, he will be dead. You can think of it as a roundabout way of exacting revenge if you need."

Ralmeath groaned, powerful and terrifying.

"I was getting to that, Ral." Kaem turned back to Quistix, moving closer as if the next part was a secret. "The other night, we saw something else. Some sort of red-eyed apparition. One of our sources called it a *Crimson Soul Reaper*. It wafted over the palace gates and started roaming around here. It attacked a young ewanian girl in the woods." Her eyes had fear in them. "*I saw it*, Lux. That thing ripped her off the ground, right into the air!

Tortured her for *hours*. He says they feed off *fear*. It seemed like it was growing *stronger* as it abused her. In the morning, when it grew tired of her, it dropped her head-first onto our campfire. I can still hear her screams when I try to sleep, Q." Kaem winced, eyes closed at the recollection.

"By the Gods...this is insane." Quistix shook her head and tucked a dark curl behind her pointed ear.

"We've been hearing tortured screams of animals every night, finding remains that are... *they're a real mess*. I've tried to shoot it with arrows, but it doesn't seem phased. Omen says that because they're created with black magic, light magic is the only way to combat them. That's why we summoned you."

"How did you know I could do magic at all?" Quistix was shocked.

"Are you crazy? The people in Destoria talk! And I'm always there to listen with my ear to the ground. Very little happens around here that I don't eventually catch wind of through the grapevine. You forget I'm paid to investigate. I knew you were headed to Apex, too. I hope you learned a thing or two while you were there because we need a real miracle right now."

It made sense.

Even at the tavern, Kaem seemed to know a lot about her private life.

"One of our inside men says she's got about a dozen of those things still inside, at last count. If *one* can do this much damage, I shudder to think of what a handful more would do. If they get out, it's going to be *chaos*. Most of these hardworking folk around here aren't like us. They don't fight. They won't stand a chance."

Quistix glowered at Twitch, furious to be put in a position where she had to work alongside the men responsible for taking Danson from her. "What do you think?"

"I," he cleared his throat, "I think I didn't lose a child, so I can't imagine how you're feeling. But I know I don't want to stand around and do nothing while these things ravage Destoria if I really do have the chance to make a difference now."

Kaem softened, her round, black eyes bulging with sincerity. "Now that Ceosteol's free and basically *unchecked* by Exos, she's making more. Collecting parts. One of our insiders said she's got soldiers exhuming graves for remains so she can tinker and play. If those things get out, if she keeps creating these monstrosities, this whole thing will tear Destoria apart. No city will be safe. Her soul is bound to all of them. Exos and Vervaine too, from what I've heard. We've got to stop Ceosteol. We've got to cut the head off the snake."

"So… what's your plan?" Quistix looked at the crude sketch on a piece of parchment as Kaem unfurled it. The group gathered around one side of the table, staring intently at the drawing.

"Well, we've got two men on the inside helping us coordinate an attack: Omen and Arias. Arias is an akiah and has been promoted to head of the royal guard. He knew something was strange weeks ago when Vervaine returned from her imprisonment. She hasn't acted normal since. He said Exos has been acting strange, too. So Omen and he banded with us to strike while the iron's hot.

Arias can't stand to see Vervaine in this condition. He cared for her. He's agreed to help lead the royal guards away during our strike with a phony excuse. That way, we don't have to fight Destorian soldiers, too."

"Great. This task sounds tough enough as it is." Aurora chimed in. In the background, quiet, faraway fits of pleom laughter filled the air, and she smiled a little. The sound warmed her heart.

"Omen made us a map of the castle to help us navigate. It seems our best approach is to divide and conquer. Since you're the only one with magical abilities, you should be the one to seek out Ceosteol. Her lair is said to be here." She pressed a claw to the hand-drawn map.

"Currently, Vervaine is in town for some sort of public address she made today about the dikeeka trade. So it's not just Exos that we have to deal with. It could be her, too. It seems like the cover of night and the element of surprise would give us our only advantages. We have a real shot if we rest tonight, prepare our weapons, and review the plan again. If we wait and attack tomorrow night, cover ourselves with soot, and stay silent, we will be in good shape. There's also the matter of Hadina's armor..."

"What do you mean?"

"She was a powerful wizard, like you, adept in fire magic. She was entombed in her fortified armor."

Suddenly, Quistix recalled what Thaxyl said at Uvege's in Apex, and it all struck her like lightning, chilling her blood instantly. "Someone told me about it in the floating city."

"There's an entrance up into the bowels of the palace from the far end of the crypts. It would be on your way up to Ceosteol's lair, and it could mean the difference between coming out of this alive and being a suicide mission. The only problem is our sources don't know much about the crypts or what you'll find there, beyond the palace's lower entrance, and the door leading outside appears to be locked tight."

"Twitch, do you think you could handle it?" She turned to the wyl, hopeful.

"I'd bet my life on it." He piped up.

Kaem scoffed. "You can try, but I'm not optimistic. Toughest lock I've ever seen."

"You're looking at one of the former heads of the Thieves Guild and a master at my craft. I'm happy to make a friendly wager if you don't believe me."

Kaem laughed. "I trust you."

"Splitting up, though? Is that *wise*?" Quistix doubted the plan.

Kaem sighed. "The way I see it, if we all head for Ceosteol, then Exos and Vervaine will be free to try to gather troops and retaliate."

"Let's say tomorrow, Twitch is able to get us in there. If I'm supposed to go in through the crypts, what'll you do?"

"Ralmeath and I planned to go in top-side. Aurora should go with us. I've heard the crypt gets narrow in spots, and I don't think her horns will make it either. I plan to grapple up the side of the north tower and open the gate for the others. This way, once we are in the palace, we can hit them from both sides. Attack from the top and bottom.

We could seek out Exos and Vervaine, and you could smoke out Ceosteol. We would hopefully meet you in the middle somewhere, down near the dungeon level where she's keeping her undead little *toys*." Kaem tapped a talon on the dungeon illustration on the parchment.

"Will it be locked?" Quistix asked. "Will the door from the crypt up to the dungeon be locked from the other side? I don't want us to get trapped down there and not be able to help you because we are stuck in some underground graveyard."

Kaem's expression went blank. "I… I don't know. I'm sorry. This has all been a lot to coordinate." Kaem's feathers fluffed. "I'm sure it will be, and if it's anything like the one in the crypt, we might have to meet you there and try to unlock it for the other side if we can."

Aurora stepped forward. "In Apex, I read about a spell that might also help you gain entry even if it is locked," Aurora added. "I could teach it to you tonight if you'd like."

"Absolutely." Quistix didn't even think about it. Her citrine eyes glistened in the light of the campfire as she looked back to Kaem. "I hate the idea of us all splitting up. Seems unwise to divide our forces."

"You need that armor if you're going to stand a chance with Exos or Ceosteol. They're long-time practicing mages. You need every advantage this world has to offer right now. Arrows, whips, and axes are great, but we are going up against some *real* power here. Power that can render our weapons useless with the bat of an eye. This is why I sent for you. Your wild magic gives us the edge we need to put a stop to this. If you can find any other way, I'm listening."

A silence fell upon them for a moment. Quistix knew the quichyrd was right and trusted her. Her shrewd fighting strategies had gotten her this far. She'd heard many successful battle stories throughout the years as Kaem purchased and repaired weapons with her in Bellaneau. She idolized the quichyrd for her bravery and the calm, strategic manner in which she approached danger. Her feathered gooseflesh bore few scars. In the decades she'd known the woman, she'd always lived to tell the tale.

"I know you care about everyone here, and you're about to try to talk them out of this, but we need all hands on deck right now. This is our only shot, Quistix. Win or lose, everyone here is willing to fight for this cause today. *Right?*"

Twitch and Aurora nodded confidently. Ralmeath opened her wide maw and roared in enthusiastic agreement. Kaem raised an eyebrow at Quistix.

"What do you say, old friend? Want to save Destoria?"

39

*Newberry Ranch,
Outskirts of Desdemona,
Willowdale*

The howl of symphs shattered the silence of the farm. Thunder rumbled in the distance. A scorched wooden fence post staked upright in the ground seemed to mock Quistix through its glowering grooves. Pinching her eyes shut, Quistix tried to calm the chaos raging inside of her. Stifled fear, uncertainty, and nerves sloshed in her stomach, swirling into a potent cocktail of seething anger.

Sparks danced from her fingertips as a flame-filled her palm. Quistix opened her eyes and hurled her palms toward the squat post, sending a pitiful flame twirling forward, fizzling out before it touched the charred surface.

"Harness your power," Aurora called out from a distance, disrupting her delicate concentration. Her fur-covered face peeked out at Quistix from behind the protection of a donik tree. Quistix flicked her finger, dropping her hands and shoulders as Aurora spoke again. "Utilize your training."

Quistix glared back at her through the deceptive shadows of dusk. She turned back toward the fence and gritted her teeth, biting back the words. Fear fluttered in her belly at the thought of the momentous battle to come.

Now was the time to rise to glory

Or fail. Losing everyone she had grown to care for in the process.

Crushing anxiety squeezed the air from her lungs. Deep within, she was raw, hollow. The empty pit in her chest called to her, dragging her thoughts back to Danson and the raging house fire that began it all.

Struggling to refocus, she fluttered her fingers as she had practiced. In the palm of her hand, she summoned sparks. She watched the pitiful flame slowly grow, then shrink and die again.

"Feel your power welling up inside of you. Release it." Aurora chirped again.

Quistix clamped her hands into fists and whipped around to face Aurora. "What does that even mean? I am trying to focus!"

Aurora stepped out from behind the tree trunk, her gaze innocent and apologetic. "It's... what the books said."

"Do the books say to yammer when I'm trying to practice? Right now, *here*, *this* is life or death! If I don't figure this out," she groaned and spun. "You memorized the words, but you have no idea what you are talking about! So stop!"

Aurora's neck elongated and stiffened. "I could be of help if you'd just *listen* to me. I have read dozens of texts on destruction magic. Tomes on every kind, in fact! I can recite to you its history from its conception until–"

"Have you cast a *single* spell?" Quistix interrupted, eyebrow cocked in smug condescension.

"The worthy are not always chosen," she said with melancholic pride, "and the chosen are not always *worthy*."

"Oh, you think *you* are more worthy?" Quistix crossed her arms.

Aurora puffed out a breath of frustration and paused. "*I think* you are scared and frustrated. You're under immense pressure, distracted, and flooded with emotion. Instead of harnessing it and using it for your craft, you are using it to start a fight with me."

Quistix's scowl softened. "You're right." She walked back to the tree and folded her arms over a chest-high branch. "I swore I was done with this nonsense. I just wanted a life. Something simple and honest. I never wanted *this*."

Aurora thought for a moment, and, for the first time, she put herself in Quistix's position. "I understand. I'm not here to tell you that peace is always possible. However, I can say with certainty that you were given unique gifts. We don't always get the gifts we *want*, but we get the gifts we were *made for. You*, Quistix Daedumal, were born to be a fierce wielder of magic. I am grateful to have beings like you who stand up for what they believe is right instead of hiding away in the forest forever, forgoing life entirely."

Quistix blinked a few times, taken aback. "Was that… your attempt at *encouragement*?"

Aurora grinned. "How did I do?"

Quistix chuckled. "It wasn't half bad."

"Now is the time to fight. That is not something a Medallion of Focus or any training can do for you. Magic is a fickle, unforgiving weapon. So you have to make a choice. Are you in this wholeheartedly? Or do we tuck tail and run?"

Quistix thought of Danson. His limp body lying in the snow. The heart-piercing pain that it brought to mind.

How many other parents are to suffer the same fate? How many other children might die if I hide away now?

"After trekking across Destoria, I am tired. Tired of *running*. Have you something from the dark recesses of that library to help me concentrate? If so, I am all ears." Quistix held the tip of her pointed ear forward.

"Close your eyes for a moment."

Quistix shot a look of uncertainty but reluctantly closed her eyes.

"Try to listen to your heartbeat."

Beyond the whirl of thoughts, Quistix listened intently for the rhythmic thumping.

"Focus on the beat in your fingertips and toes."

As though a barrier had been placed between her and her senses, Quistix broke through the thin veil in her mind and felt the throbbing in her fingers and toes.

"That beat is always there. It was there since you took your first breath. It will be there until your last. It never leaves. It never quits. You need only listen. When chaos rages, your heart drums onward, uninterrupted."

Quistix's shoulders relaxed. Her heart rate slowed. Tension in her neck and hands melted away, and the thrumming of her heart grew louder than ever before. "Remember what your Professor Teryl said about controlling your mind?"

"*Either you control it, or it controls you*'" Quistix mimicked Teryl's Apexian accent.

"Yes! *Focus*. Use your energy to show us what you are feeling."

A warm glow emanated from Quistix, lighting up her veins and washing her skin in golden light. She opened her eyes as they changed from citrine to a deeper, burnt orange. Fluttering her fingers, sparks spiraled in her palm, igniting into a solid, steady flame. She thrust her palm forward, launching a fireball.

The sun-faded fence post ignited, ablaze with crackling fire.

Quistix swirled her fingers, and a flurry of frost puffed out like a cloud of fractals, smothering the flames and freezing the post solid. It shimmered in a glistening, pale blue sheen from the layer of ice encasing it.

With her other hand, she reached toward a thick branch that had fallen beside Aurora.

Outstretching her fingers, Quistix raised her hand into the air and swished it past herself. The branch flung across the field and *thwacked* against the post. The frozen wood shattered like exploding glass in different directions.

Aurora stared mouth agape, in utter amazement. "Amazing! Do another!"

Whirling her hands over her head, the wind twisted like a cyclone, creating dust devils in the air.

"Again!" Aurora shouted, bouncing up and down, giddy with excitement.

Oozing with power, Quistix thought for a moment and lifted her hands. Water from the aquifer below bubbled up, flooding the grass. It swirled and splashed, creating a wave that flowed swiftly, splashing Aurora's hooves.

The esteg panicked. Her hooves sunk into the muddied ground. The tree above her swayed violently in the wind. She heard a *snap*. Then a *pop*. She looked down to see the tree roots tug themselves from the water-logged soil.

"Quistix, that's enough," her anxious voice hollered over the whipping wind.

But Quistix was hyper-focused, almost in a trance. She lifted twigs and branches and shards of the exploded fence post into the whirling winds.

Aurora shouted in fear of the airborne projectiles smacking into the tree beside her, embedding themselves into its trunk. The tree snapped as the roots freed from the ground.

Quistix was able to snap herself out of it at the sound of Aurora's terrified cries. She sprinted toward the esteg, knocking her out of the way of the falling tree, smashing them both into a squishy puddle of muck inches away from the deadly downed trunk. The sound of the donik crashing down was brief and as deafening as the riotous thunder cracking overhead. Quistix pressed herself up in the slop, freshly washed obsidian cotton shirt now caked with soggy, brown mud.

Another zap of distant lightning lit up the sky. Hefty rain droplets began to pelt down, stinging them with their weighty impact.

"Are you alright?" Quistix asked in a panic as the leaves fluttered around them.

"I… think so," Aurora answered as she lifted her head.

Quistix gasped, staring at the mud behind her. Following the elf's gaze, Aurora looked back at her trapped antlers peeking out of the mire several feet away from them both. The awkward silence grew as the gravity of the situation settled in, both staring at the shorn horns in bewilderment.

After the shock faded, Aurora spoke. "You know," her tone was eerily calm, "you never *have* been one for good timing."

40

*The Ruby Palace Crypts,
Desdemona,
Willowdale*

The three full moons lit the plaque on the mausoleum door, which read:

*Within lies a traitor of magic,
A master of Destruction.
Claiming the lives of over 500
In the Great Fire of Willowdale,
For eternity, those lost souls
Now haunt her tomb.
DO NOT ENTER.*

It was locked, just as Kaem suggested. Twitch clasped his paws together and popped his knuckles as if to say, "Stand back, I'll handle this." With his homemade lock-pick set, he inserted several small items into the keyhole below the handle. Quistix kept a watchful eye out over the field, searching for anyone who may have spotted them despite their lurking in the shadows cloaked in black fabric. With her back pressed hard to Twitch's, she could feel the writhing of his shoulder blades as he maneuvered the picks with an almost alarming amount of ease. She had no doubt that no lock in Destoria could keep the determined wyl out if he wanted in. Despite his jovial, silly personality, he had never falsely advertised his abilities.

Click.

The quiet, metallic noise rang out into the ominous, hazy night sky.

"Ha! Toughest lock she's ever seen? Pffft!" He scoffed. "Never send a quichyrd for a wyl's job," his voice filled with the utmost satisfaction, trying hard not to gloat further. He tugged at the handle, and a puff of old air and dust wafted out of the mausoleum toward them. He rolled out his arm, allowing her to enter past him. "Warriors first, madame."

Inside, three stone coffins sat along the walls among a twisted mass of overgrown tree roots that had invaded through the dirt floor. Twitch walked to the first casket and wiped a metal plate bolted to the stone, reading the inscription aloud. "Annabeth Tempest"

"How do I know which one is the right one?" Quistix found herself grinding her molars in frustration.

"Maybe we just open them all and see if *any* have armor inside."

Quistix knelt next to one and looked at the engraving. "No, I think this is it. There is no name, just *'The Shame of Destoria.'*"

"Yeah?" Twitch hopped over a grave to stand next to her.

Quistix shoved the top of the coffin, but the stone slab didn't budge. "Help me get this thing open." They shoved their shoulders into the slab, forcing it to move. As they grunted and strained together, the stone top crashed to the other side, shaking the stone floor of the crypt.

Twitch looked away. "Is it her?"

"There's no corpse. Look!"

He peered into the coffin. The bottom was missing. Below was a small landing and stairs leading downward.

"I'm going down." Quistix removed her pack and set it at the side of the grave. Digging around in its contents, she pulled out *Swordbreaker* and lowered herself into the hole carefully, dropping to the platform below.

Twitch grabbed his bow and quiver and hopped nimbly over the side, landing almost silently on the soft pads of his feet.

Quistix led the way to a sharp corner at the end of the tunnel's hallway. A charred being stood with its back to them in tattered burlap clothing. Quistix's boot crunched sand and dust against the stone floor beneath her despite her careful steps.

The being whirled around and lunged at her. Before she could think, she reacted, slashing at it with her double-headed ax, hacking through its flesh. Bones snapped and fractured. Coagulated blood dribbled like thick syrup from the wound.

Its dead eyes glared, still occasionally blinking. It came at her again, thrashing its gnarled body through the air at her.

Twitch fired an arrow that pierced its temple.

She hit it with the ax a second time. This time in the throat. The head lopped off, coal-black eyes fixed on her. Its body collapsed to the floor, jerking wildly.

"What the hell is that thing?!" Quistix tried to concentrate despite the chomping and snarling of the severed head.

Unable to muster his voice, Twitch shrugged, eyes wild with terror.

They carefully walked on the far edge of the hall, narrowly avoiding its chomping jaws.

After another short corridor, they approached a craggy entrance to a cave-like room, walls lined with blazing animal-fat torches. Inside, dozens of benches sat parallel, like pews, facing a raised rock. Several were filled with black-eyed, burlap-clad attendees.

It was an underground church.

Quistix shivered at the dark nature of the services that seemed to be held there. Atop the raised, crimson-splattered rock sat a podium and an ornate tomb resting beneath a larger-than-life statue of a praying woman. The flickering torch fire gave her face an eerie glow. The tomb looked more like a sacrificial altar. Perhaps it had many uses.

Two nearly nude women with blackened, peeling skin chanted in unison in front of the tomb, wearing little beyond their burlap skirts, flanked by torches on poles just taller than themselves. Behind the ladies, a red-robed figure grabbed a carved staff adorned with a polished stone orb and moved toward the edge of the stone plateau.

"The darkness welcomes you." A delicate feminine hand outstretched from beneath the billowing sleeve of the robe.

The crowd chanted Latin, low and in perfect unison.

"Who are you?" Twitch said, his voice sounding brave despite the trembling of his hands.

"*Hadina Tempest.* Once a respected queen of the *living*, now a besmirched hostage of *darkness*." She listened to the silence that befell the room as if receiving a transmission. She smiled and nodded. "The voices tell me you've come with *the Illuminator.*"

Hadina's eyes glimmered green at its very mention, framed by long locks of jet-black hair.

There it was again. That damned Illuminator...

"I haven't figured out what it is yet." Quistix lifted her eyes to meet Hadina's creepy gaze. "How do you know I have it?"

"I hear Eldrin discussing it." Hadina's words echoed off the cave walls. She seemed to be hearing a voice that was not there.

Shocked at the mention of her father, Quistix studied Hadina's glowing green eyes. "How do you know Eldrin?"

Hadina chuckled a little. "We're old friends. Your father was a close friend to my husband in life,

King Colton Tempest of Destoria. Eldrin was working on a resurrection spell, dabbling in the black and blood magics. Colton heard the rumors and sent for him. Since black magic is so easily detected in Apex, he was summoned to Desdemona so that they may share their findings in the privacy of the Ruby Palace. Colton spared no expense when he arrived. Eldrin was to teach him his techniques in advanced healing in exchange for my husband's and his quichyrd's findings on resurrection. They exchanged information every night for months until Lura found out she was pregnant with her second. Eldrin rushed home to be with you and Lura, tome full of notes in tow. After Lura's death, Eldrin was scheduled to return but never showed up. Colton sent him letters by symph, ordering him to come back and finish their research. Your father didn't reply. When Colton heard Eldrin tried to sacrifice you to save Lura, he was livid."

As Hadina tipped her staff, Quistix felt her mind go blank. Twitch wrapped his arms around her as her eyes rolled back into her head. She gasped and swayed on her feet.

The elf felt trapped inside of her memories, unable to control what was happening. Merely a spectator watching moments unfold in front of her.

Everything went black.

41

*The Ruby Palace,
Desdemona,
Willowdale*

The night was going to be long and arduous, this much Kaem could tell as she approached the castle walls with Ralmeath, Frok, and Dally. Ralmeath made her way up the meadow in the shadows, no easy feat for a hefty, snow-white Bramolt bear. Frok and Dally buzzed up ahead, staring in opposite directions while the bear hid amongst the thick, bare apple trees in the orchard behind the estate. She buried her furry body among tufts of high, dead grass.

They signaled, when the coast was clear, to pass to a closer tree or duck behind a roll of hay.

Though there was no snow in Willowdale at the moment, the temperatures were frigid, stiffening the fauna into crinkled brown corpses that sounded like wax paper crunching with every step. Kaem cursed herself for not anticipating the amount of noise Ralmeath would make simply getting to the castle. A rookie mistake she hoped would not cost them dearly.

Kaem watched as the palace guards patrolled the upper level between the spires. As Ralmeath and the others joined her at the palace gates, she gave a hand signal to the pleoms. They nodded and flitted into the top of a stripped apple tree, hiding among the empty symph nests. Kaem freed her grapple from her thick belt. Oddly enough, parts of it had been forged by Quistix years before, in what seemed like her previous life as a mother and blacksmith.

Frok waved a scaled wing wildly, and Kaem shot the bolt over the fence. The forked end clattered against the stone walkway of the empty courtyard, and she winced at the commotion overhead as a guard shuffled his way over toward them to find the source of the racket.

She pulled carefully, dragging the prong to the gate, catching it on the lip at the top, nearly twenty feet above her. She tugged the line taut and lay down in the grass. She could feel her cold blood pulse through her body as the guard waltzed past, satisfied that the noise was not a concern. Dally waved, and Kaem wasted no time. She tugged tight on the rope and placed her boots on the gate. She was angry that though being bird-like in nature, she, *like all quichyrds*, was not born with the ability to fly. However, she was, indeed, thankful that she weighed almost as little as a bird. A stiff wind could knock her over, but she kept herself weighed down with weapons, armor, and footwear that had flat plates of metal sewn into the soles. As she crawled up the rope, she was grateful that she could do so with ease. She reached the top, pocketed her hook, and scuttled down the other side of the fence until landing in a grassy patch near the stone path with a *plop*.

She signaled the pleoms, and they fluttered around in different directions, doing a perimeter check. As soon as one of the guards overhead made his way behind the wall of the spire, Dally did a flip in the air.

Kaem shook her head at the dragonling's inability to be serious in such a dire time for the isle. In such a dire time for *them*. She scuttled over to the palatial gate entrance, quickly unlocking each from a series of seven bolts. She struggled with the last one as Ralmeath crept to the gate. Kaem could hear the guard's armored feet click along the open stone bridge between the ruby-capped spires.

Ralmeath winced in anticipation as she pressed the thick, ornate metal door. The right gate groaned open with a rusted creak. The iron hinges called out like the squeal of a small noubald being dragged to the slaughterhouse.

Kaem cursed quietly into the frigid night air as soon as the footsteps halted. The guard above shouted, "Sir, the grounds have been breached!"

The stomping of more than a dozen feet clattered along the stone bridge as macho human and barbarian men stumbled into full view, chests puffed beneath their royal ruby-encrusted armor.

But Kaem and the others had prepared for this, having heard the gate squeal countless times during intelligence-gathering expeditions. They debated pouring oil into the hinges, but several were far too high to reach, so instead, they embraced it, knowing it would call full attention to them.

They were all in their stances. One they had practiced in repetition drills the hours before. Kaem and Ralmeath stood, arrows loaded in their bows, pointing at the guards. Frok and Dally worked in tandem, nearly mimicking each other, pulling clawfuls of grass-laden raakaby feces from the burlap sacks slung around Kaem and Ralmeath's shoulders and molding them around the arrowheads. Almost in unison, they fluttered backward and vomited streams of fire at the dung, lighting the ends ablaze.

"Fire!" Kaem's voice was more of a war cry than a command, eyes locked on her metal-plated human target.

Together, the long-time pair fired their shots. Both flaming arrows landed. Kaem's into the human's bearded face, Ralmeath's into the side of a barbarian who had been reaching up into his quiver to load his own bow. Both men squealed in pain, sending a shock wave of fear to the surrounding men. Kaem and Ralmeath were busy reloading when the human flung himself over the back of the bridge, landing on his back. The sound of his final breath echoed around the stone walls as his face crackled like a campfire, with a straightened piece of donik coming straight up like a pole without a flag. Flames licked the shimmering emerald-black quichyrd feathers on the back.

Ralmeath's victim spun, instead, in circles, trying to pull the flaming arrow from his ribcage, setting the two humans beside him on fire with the moving inferno biting through his hair and furry clothing tufted out between the seams of his chest and back plates.

By the time the other men realized it was too late for their fellow barbarian, Kaem and Ralmeath had another arrow locked and loaded, and Frok and Dally were firing up another load of grassy scat.

"Fire!" Kaem shouted again.

Ralmeath roared as their barrage of blazing arrows made their way into doomed targets, piercing tender muscles, and blistering skulls.

42

*Student Dormitories,
Institute of Magic,
Apex City,
Apex*

They were at Eldrin's desk. Quistix was just a child. Eldrin pointed to a passage in his tome.

She peered at the book.

"I can't read it. The words are too hard."

"What's this word?" Her father's voice said, sounding like warm honey in her ears, soothing her with nostalgia.

"The," she squeaked. "Ill-oom-in-ate-or?"

"That's right! Now say it fast."

"Ill-uminator!"

"You are gonna be smarter than your mom and I put together, kid." He squeezed her four-year-old frame tightly. *"Do you want to know what an Illuminator is? It means something that brings light. Like you do for me and Mom. You bring so much light, Quistix. You are our little* Illuminator.*"*

The Underground Church, The Ruby Palace Crypts, Desdemona, Willowdale

A shock zapped Quistix, seizing her body in Twitch's clutches as she came to, the blackness momentarily dissipating.

"I... I'm it? Is it me?" Quistix asked uneasily, unable to control the shaking of her hands. "I'm *the Illuminator*?"

"Yes." All the beings in the room hissed in near-perfect unison, including Hadina.

The blackness enveloped her again, and she fell as limp as a washrag in the wyl's embrace. She was transported in time to another crystal-clear memory, replayed without the ravages of time vividly.

43

*Eldrin's Dormitory,
Institute of Magic,
Apex City,
Apex*

The elven child pretended to sleep while her parents argued. Though she could not see them, their muffled voices were intelligible through the covers.

"No, Eldrin. I can't allow this."

It was Lura. Mother. Oh, how she missed the sound of her mother's voice after all these years...

Eldrin's voice startled her. "Lura, we have the chance to eradicate death! This changes everything. How could this possibly be a bad thing?"

"It involves black magic! You'll get us kicked out of Apex, and that's not even the worst part of it! She's our daughter. She's just a little girl! You can't just use her like a tool! She's a person, not a pawn."

"She's meant for a far greater purpose than protection spells and parlor-trick illusions. She can halt mortality, Lura! Every beloved husband, every child taken too soon, every mother robbed of her life by illness... she can bring them back!"

"No! It won't be them*! They'll be... wrong. There's a* reason *black magic is banned. You tangle with something dark when you disrupt what lies beyond the Ether. It's not right!"*

"You haven't seen the devastation I have in the healing ward. People beyond a cure. Innocent people who I can't mend with magic. This Lura... is possibly the most important discovery of our time. And you want me to just let it be*? None of this works without Quistix, without her light. Without her pure power. If there was any way I could do this without her, I would."*

"You'd be robbing her life to save others. This is your daughter. Your own flesh and blood!

She heard her father sigh, long and loud.

"I know you can find another way. Promise me you'll try."

Eldrin's voice croaked, "Alright!"

44

*The Underground Church,
Ruby Palace Crypts,
Desdemona,
Willowdale*

Quistix collapsed to the floor, slipping from the wyl's arms, eyes fluttering, body limp.

The unfamiliar, unassailable presence that had inhabited her mind was gone. Disoriented, she saw the black-eyed beings seated in the pews surrounding them. The words on the door of the crypt swam in her skull:

For eternity, those lost souls haunt her tomb.

"Are they… the people who died in your fire?" Her voice was hoarse, mouth dry. She trembled as she stood, feeling weakened by the witch's magic.

"*My* fire?" Hadina scoffed, squinting beneath the hood of the robe. "I started no fire. I killed no one. It was *him*. Everyone around Colton Tempest was always cannon fodder. We were all pawns in a jealous king's evil little game."

"I don't understand." She lifted a hand to her aching head and attempted to stand without Twitch's aid.

Hadina continued. "Years of his abuse and torture drove me nearly to the brink of madness. Then I bore children, two beautiful girls, and he bestowed the punishments on our daughters as well. I was too afraid to retaliate, that is until the day he nearly killed our eldest. She was always a *wicked* child. His seething black magic corrupted her with its insidious grip the moment she was born. One day, after she nearly burned her younger sister alive in a shack, Colton made crimson soul reapers torture her for days. Then he ordered his quichyrd lackey to strip our baby of her powers for good. The abuse nearly broke me as a mother."

Quistix was enthralled by the tale, much of it sounding like familiar rumors she'd heard as a girl in Bellaneau.

"I left on foot to rally forces to overthrow him. And I did. By the time the thousand brave souls were ready to storm the castle, he had set fire to the kingdom. *Our* kingdom. Men, women, and children all burned in their beds as the fire spread out of control. His men finally found me at Grim Harbor. I was captured. Held prisoner in the caverns below the palace like some grimy dungeon rat. Colton told my daughters they could torture me... or join me. Exos obliged willingly, but Vervaine was nearly beaten to death by Colton before she finally laid a hand on me. After three long weeks, weeks that felt like an *eternity*... I was dead. *We* were dead." She spread her arms wide, motioning to the dead-eyed parishioners.

"I reside here now, along with these faithful, smoldering spirits of the long-forgotten. Our mortal remains banished from the mainland. Colton couldn't bear to look at them."

Hadina tilted her staff toward the elf, stunning her. Transporting her elven mind to a different place and time where she hazily viewed the world...

Through *Hadina's* eyes.

45

*Dungeon of the Ruby Palace,
Desdemona,
Willowdale*

Hadina was chained to the wall in the leaking bowels of the stone building, a constant *drip-drip-drip* of water beside her driving her insane.

An onyx-haired child stood before her, smeared with blood.

Hadina's blood.

The girl skewered a dagger into her mother's chest, twisting.

Hadina threw her head back and screamed, her lifeblood escaping her.

There was a sadistic smile creeping up into her youthful cheeks. She leaned in and whispered in her mother's ear. "*The darkness welcomes you, mother.*"

Everything grew dark.

So *quiet*.

So *still*.

So *cold*.

A gentle orange glow cut through the black, growing its shining beam into a blinding force. Hadina's inflexible eyelids opened with difficulty. Her unforgiving body was icy, stiff with rigor.

Young Exos was gone. In her place, a kneeling quichyrd with glowing green eyes examined her rigid form carefully. A sick grin formed on the corners of her beak.

"Welcome back to us."

46

The Underground Church,
The Ruby Palace Crypts,
Desdemona,
Willowdale

Quistix was released from the spell once again, speechless at what she'd witnessed. Hadina brushed aside a tuft of her long, flowing hair. Her luminous green eyes locked on the elf and wyl before her. She was a true elven beauty, though her full lips showed no trace of a smile.

Quistix tried to ignore the hundreds of coal-black eyes of Hadina's minions burning into her. "I assume you believe, because I'm the *Illuminator*, that I can somehow bring you back from the dead?"

"I'm already back from the dead." She sneered. "I need *finality*. *We* need finality. You are the mage we need, powerful and full of light magic." Hadina said, her voice smooth as honey, "the one with the ability to end this limbo for good. You have the ability to bring us to life. Or to end our suffering. We are but tentacles, though you have the weapon to cut the head off the octopus."

"I wouldn't *begin* to know how to do that!" Her head was swimming. She felt so frazzled by everyone's trumped-up beliefs in her. They had no grip on reality. The *real* reality. She was just a homeless widow from Bellaneau. No son. No forge. No money. It was baffling why everyone regarded her as the key to something so vastly important in this life and *beyond*.

"Eldrin took studious notes when he and Colton were experimenting. Your father was brilliant. He had a near-mastery of resurrection magic and noted everything in his book," she extended her pale hand. "Bring me his tome, and we may begin."

With great hesitation, Quistix reached into her satchel and produced her father's magnum opus, worn and frayed just as the man's psyche had been when he'd written in it. She ushered it up to one of the women beside Hadina, who resumed staring into the distance with her dead, raven-black eyes after handing it off.

"I think the part you're looking for has been taken. Some pages were removed long before I took possession." Quistix shivered at the cold dankness seeping into her black cloak.

Hadina rifled her fingers through the pages, flipping quickly through the sections, her eyes blazing neon, the book basking in their glow. She touched the torn shards, the fragments of pages where the resurrection spell had been shorn with abandon.

She held her hand over the book and concentrated. *"Quae quondam erat redi."*

As the words oozed from her plump lips, fresh pages sprouted from the torn shards like budding leaves from a tree, unfurling before her, replacing the missing pieces of parchment. Though less yellowed than the rest of the pages, they matched the size and shape of the surrounding ones perfectly.

Words and sketches started to appear like ink through a napkin.

"Good as new." The satisfied smile on Hadina's face said it all. Her spell *worked.*

"Here we are. It says Eldrin's resurrection spell requires one voluntary sacrifice of someone with great light magic powers, *i.e., the Illuminator.* The soul must be obtained by a willing participant. This is the main distinction between Eldrin's method and a traditional, black magic resurrection."

"What about the repercussions? You know, of casting it? You heard what my mother said," Quistix pointed behind her, though her mother was nowhere in sight. "You wouldn't be *you.* They wouldn't be themselves either."

"There are thousands of us here. Wandering restlessly. Existing aimlessly, our souls filled with woe and darkness instead of life and vigor." Hadina growled, her voice powerful yet somehow desperate.

Pleading, almost. "We can't *rest*, but worse, we can't *live*. Doomed to wander as puppets controlled by a sick master. Screaming for help within our own minds. Pleasure no longer exists. We move, we breathe, but we are not *living*. We need to be released from this decaying purgatory. For decades, I have patiently waited for someone like you, with your power, to deliver us from this fate. The undead all around Destoria will bend a knee at the thought of you, statues erected in nearly every city in the isle. Songs will be sung of you. You will leave behind a legacy of something good. Something pure."

"But only if I make a voluntary sacrifice?"

Hadina nodded. "You can rejoin Danson."

The very utterance of his name from her lips made Quistix want to crumble to the cold dirt below her and hide beneath her midnight-black cloak.

"He waits for his mother beyond the Ether." Hadina sounded *kind*, her voice soft at that moment. Like she was speaking mother-to-mother. "He hopes you'll do the right thing for all of us."

"This doesn't feel right at *all*, Q," Twitch muttered, snapping her out of her dream-like haze. "Danson wouldn't want you to kill yourself."

Quistix couldn't even blink. She felt dazed at the idea. "I could bring them all back, Twitch."

"You don't *know* that!" The wyl was suddenly the voice of reason. "You're going to believe some dead witch in a crypt? No disrespect to your father or anything, but this could all just be some lunatic's *science experiment*. Stick with the plan! We have to cut the head off the snake. That's *Ceosteol*. Don't forget why we're here." He nodded toward the tomb full of armor.

"She can hear every word you say, you know." Hadina's eyes glowed green. Quistix and Twitch had not even seen them change colors.

Her voice was not her own. It had morphed into something inhuman. Something... *darker*.

Older.

Ancient.

"I'm everywhere." Her plump lips curled up into a wicked smile.

"No, Hadina. He's right." She snapped out of her malaise, standing proudly, firm in her decision. "I can't do that. This isn't the way."

Hadina's smile dropped, and the dozens of unfeeling faces followed suit, their grins turning to cold grimaces.

"Hadina isn't here anymore." The voice came from the woman and all the black-eyed beings in unison, like a chorus of youthful demons.

The woman erupted in a hearty laugh. The beings all did the same. It was a wild cacophony of sick laughter bouncing off the claustrophobic dirt walls.

What once was Hadina stepped toward them. The other beings did the same, all closing in on them in a solitary, eerie motion, like undead soldiers.

They blinked hundreds of black eyes in perfect unison. One single, furious, connected mass.

And then they all raced toward her.

47

*The Underground Church,
The Ruby Palace Crypts,
Desdemona,
Willowdale*

"**B***ulla subsisto!*" Quistix screamed, her eyes starting to morph into another color. Her outward-turned palms sizzled a little, but her concentration remained focused on the spirit of Hadina and the black-eyed beings under her command.

"Got any ideas, Twitch?" Quistix had her arms out, creating one of the magical barriers she'd learned from Professor Teryl. The wyl was in awe of her newfound skill. His furry mouth hung open in shock at her sudden display of magical ability, though short-lived due to the danger lurking mere feet from them.

Enraged black-eyed beings beat their young fists against the walls of her barrier, mouths dripping with foamy, black drool, climbing atop each other to find a vulnerable spot and gain access to her and the wyl.

The torchlight dimmed, blocked by stacking bodies, encasing them in a darkened dome.

"Can the barrier move with you?"

"I think so!" Quistix tried to move in any direction, but felt an incredible force pushing back. She tried again, throwing her body weight into the direction of the tunnel beyond the tomb.

Same result.

Quistix shook her head, panic and fear settling into her gut. Vicious beings scrambled onto the shoulders of others, clumsily bashing the barrier with furious fists.

Twitch watched as an elderly black-eyed woman glared hungrily at him through the blockade, her mouth full of pointed teeth. Locking her inky eyes on him, her jaw unhinged slowly, and she roared. The sound of her hellish scream vibrated the darkened barrier.

The last of the light was snuffed out when another row of bodies made it to the top.

"They can't get to us," Twitch began, moving to the edge, "but maybe we can get to *them*."

He wrapped his hand around her emerald dagger handle and raised it above his head. He brought the blade down toward the elderly woman's head.

The shaft of the blade broke instantly as it burrowed into the barrier. Twitch pulled back and looked down in horror at the fractured remnants of the blade protruding from the emerald-encrusted handle. "Well, that's not gonna work!"

Twitch looked around in the darkness, peering out between the creatures, swinging arms and leg gaps. "Wait! Can you add flames to this thing?"

Quistix scrunched her face. "That's mixing fire and protection. They're two separate schools of magic. I don't know how to do that yet. This is already draining me. I can feel it. I can't keep this up."

"Well, we gotta do something. If that did this to solid steel," he held up the ruined dagger, "then arrows are just a waste."

"I'll try." She swallowed hard. "If this doesn't work," her heart felt heavy, "I just want you to know I'm glad we crossed paths."

Twitch managed to smile through the fear. "It's been an honor."

Quistix closed her glowing white eyes and imagined the feeling of rage overtaking her. She pictured the rattle she found on her father's desk, the son he had with another woman. Heat began to radiate from her skin. She pictured walls of fire flashing up around her, lapping at the stone roof above, just as the professor had taught her. She outstretched her fingers and waved her extended hands down to the floor.

She screamed.

The barrier erupted in flames, illuminating the darkness with a wild woof of orange. A teenage boy beating on the barrier in front of her ignited. His hair was engulfed in flames and smoked along with his eyebrows. He didn't cry out in pain as his skin began to peel and char. He seemed unaffected until his crispy body fell to the floor, twitching. The others followed suit. Men, women, children, and elderly forms were all curled up into scorched blackness like a hunk of meat on a campfire for far too long. The bodies started to fall away, revealing more light through the darkened dome.

The intensity on their faces never dwindled. Like melted wind-up toys, they writhed on the floor as much as their burned tendons and muscles would physically allow.

Some continued to beat on the barrier after the skin of their hands melted away.

"I've got an idea." Quistix shouted, "*Bulla evanescet!*"

With those words, the barrier dropped. Twitch's voice caught in his throat. There was nothing protecting them now from the scorched pile of trembling blackened bodies. Some tumbled inward toward them beyond where the perfect circle of the dome once was.

"*Glacies undam!*" She flexed her arms outwardly again, eyes tightly shut, deeply focused.

Twitch watched as a thick cloud of frost flowed over the beings, instantly freezing them into place with a shockwave of crystallized ice.

Hadina and the black-eyed beings were stiff.

Frozen.

Hadina stood straight at the podium, temporarily anchored in place by a layer of ice. Quistix felt her energy drain, legs wobbling beneath her. They stepped over frozen bodies and scattered, shattered, burned limbs of black-eyed beings.

Hadina's green eyes grew brighter than ever before. The torches dimmed simultaneously.

Magic was pulsing through the air. Quistix could feel it. It wasn't her own. They had to act fast.

Hadina's fingers and hands began to flex, followed soon by her face and feet.

Quistix and Twitch raced up the steps to the platform and flanked the tomb, peering down inside. Quistix marveled at what was nestled within it. A female skeleton in a flawless suit of armor.

Though the tomb was scorched, the polished silver contents inside were pristine atop the dusty skeleton of Hadina's mortal corpse, displayed in all her majesty beneath the flickering light.

A pointed helm with a faceguard shaped like a demon clutched her shriveled skull. Rounded braces were wrapped loosely around radius and ulna bones, seated perfectly beneath detailed pauldrons. The forearm vambraces were sharply pointed at the elbow tips. Obviously made for a female, the curvaceous chest piece had exquisitely carved symbols all over. The shoulders of the high-coverage breastplate jutted out sharply like splayed feathers. It tapered at the waist, overlapping cuirass attached to matching calf greaves.

More amazing than the legends had foretold, the suit was, to this skilled elven blacksmith, absolute *perfection*.

48

*The Underground Church,
The Ruby Palace Crypts,
Desdemona,
Willowdale*

The witch helped free the pieces from the dusty skeletal remains, awash with ebbing waves of nausea.

Quistix didn't hesitate to strip out of her black robe, placing the pieces on her body with both haste and reverence for the late elf. As she scrambled her way into it as quickly as her hands and feet would allow, the blacksmith in her couldn't help but appreciate every curve. She admired every skilled joint and marking.

It was a divine set made with care and patience that went beyond even her wildest childhood dreams as her grandfather's armorer's assistant. With the suit of armor complete, Quistix immediately felt a brilliant surge of energy and adrenaline rush through her veins. She snatched *Swordbreaker* and lashed it back around her waist. The cheap, worn leather belt stood out in stark contrast to the pristine armor.

The lively, ethereal version of Hadina glared at her, face now burned through the melted ice. "I'll wipe you from the isle like a stain!"

Hadina launched a fireball at Quistix, knocking her backward into several frozen beings. They shattered like porcelain into gory pieces. Quistix scrambled to her feet and sprinted to the other side of the chamber.

She launched an ice shard toward Hadina but missed. She watched as the massive bolt of ice shattered against the praying stone statue at the rear of the stage.

"You're strong but undisciplined. A wild horse yet to be broken. You remind me of my daughters." Hadina followed her with her eyes and hurled a ball of fire. Quistix changed course and dove away from it, narrowly escaping its burn. "I can do this all night. But I have a feeling you're rather fatigued."

Quistix sat with her back against a frozen black-eyed being, trying to catch her breath. Twitch pointed to the void on the right, the one they assumed would lead up to the dungeons. Quistix nodded, and they sprinted toward the other side of the cavern.

Before she could make it to the other side, Hadina struck her with a fireball that glanced off her armor. The force, however, still sent her flying, knocking her right off her feet and smashing her into the wall with a metallic clatter. Twitch tumbled toward the hole and scrambled in.

"Q, you okay?" He hollered from the hole.

"It's gonna take a lot more than that to stop me!" Quistix said, enraged. "See what you can find up there, Twitch! We have to get out of here!"

He nodded and raced up the steps to the door at the top. It was, in fact, *locked.*

"What the...?"

The lock looked complicated. It was unlike anything he had ever seen before, with a series of three dials inscribed with hieroglyphics.

49

*The Underground Church,
Ruby Palace Crypts,
Desdemona,
Willowdale*

Hadina smiled as Quistix blasted every which way with her fire-stream spell, struggling to control its directionality. The angry witch shot an ice spike toward the elf. It struck Quistix's knee, piercing the flesh. She screamed, her fire stream blinking out as she became distracted by the excruciating pain. Powering through, she quickly re-focused enough to blast Hadina with a spray of fire again.

Hadina howled in pain and darted from behind the coffin, standing below the giant iron statue of the praying woman.

Quistix concentrated, aiming her fire magic spell at the outstretched metallic face stoically suspended above the witch. Hadina closed her eyes and lifted her palms. The grotesque mounds of flesh and bone rumbled. Bones clattered and reorganized themselves.

Reassembling her fallen black-eyed beings for a resurrection.

The focused Hadina was unaware of the liquifying effigy above her until it was too late. It oozed down like silver molten lava from above, sizzling and spattering against the floor around the undead sorceress. Quistix held the fire stream steady, screaming out at the difficulty. Never taking her blazing-white irises off the dripping target. Her eyesight blurred in tandem with the exhaustion, but she couldn't stop now.

Not when they'd come this far and still had so far to go.

The liquefied iron dribbled down onto Hadina. Her last bellowing howls made Quistix cringe.

"Ahhhhhhhh!" The undead woman's hellacious scream echoed up through the chamber, chilling Twitch to his core.

Her inhuman cry finally halted, leaving the cavern of black-eyed beings in a trance-like state, staring at the walls as if they had been paused. The resurrecting bodies collapsed back into gory puddles. Hadina's molten, metal-covered corpse started to solidify. She was her own iron statue now.

A metal apparition resembling the undead witch frozen in place below a now-faceless graven idol.

Quistix yanked out the sharp shard of an icicle in the side of her knee and removed a small piece of Aurora's broken-off antler from her pocket. She scraped it against the rough side of the tomb until it ground into a pile of fine, bright green powder. She pinched it off the dirt floor and sprinkled the earthy mix onto her tongue, gagging at the taste. Within moments, she watched the hole in her knee seal closed, and the bleeding stopped. The pain still throbbed, but the miraculous closure allowed her to stand and begin rummaging through the tomb for her gorgeous prize.

Up in the cavernous bulb of the tunnel, lit by two torches near the door, Twitch studied the three-ringed lock with the hieroglyphs. He turned the outer dial until the notch above matched up with the outline of a raakaby.

Click.

Something groaned, loud and awful.

Just above his head, arrows shot from both sides of the cavern, whizzing past him with razor-sharp tips, burying themselves into the clay walls. They narrowly missed him, to the point where he felt the wind from one brush past the fur of his pointed ears.

"By the *Gods*!" He shouted, wondering if he'd wet himself in the moment. His life could have just ended, and he felt the gravity of such a silly error. He was afraid to move the dial again. As he looked around, heart slamming in his chest, he saw words carved into rigid rows lining the top of the clay walls. He squinted to read them, pulling a torch out of its holder, and spoke the words aloud. *"I have more brawn than brain."*

He looked back at the dial, realizing quickly that the glyphs were outlines of species on Destoria. He scanned his eyes around each ring. All three contained the same crude outlines: raakabys, wyls, eaflics, semdrogs, elves, ewanians, quichyrds, symphs, akiahs, barbarians—

"Barbarians!" He gasped. It was a riddle, and he knew the answer. Ducking down to avoid the arrow holes, he turned the outer dial again until the barbarian lined up with the notch.

Click, click, click! The three dials spun in different directions like a clock that had gone berserk. The door groaned, and Twitch backed up, steering well clear of any potential arrow fire. There was a quiet pause where all he could hear was Hadina growling and Quistix blasting fire like a blowtorch. Then, the top lock of the door kicked back with brute force, exposing the crack of the door beneath.

Twitch smiled. *One down, two more to go.* He was about to earn his title of master lock pick once again. He eyed the second line:

It caws and claws, but their skills give pause.

He thought for a moment.

That's *easy*. Caws and claws. They were the scourge of Destoria. *Rats of the air,* he laughed to himself. He waltzed up, cocky, to the dial and turned the middle ring to SYMPH.

WOOF! A blaze of fire blasted out of two holes below where the arrows came out, singeing the fur on his arms and the sides of his face. He screamed, dropping to the floor to quickly suffocate the flames.

"You injured, Twitch?" Quistix's voice sounded pained. She strained to keep the fire blasting.

He stood up, missing patches of fur, covered in powdery, khaki dirt. "Just my pride, my darling."

He shook it off and looked at the dial again, slumping his head. He was a buffoon. Sure, they had claws and cawed – *oh, by the Gods, did they caw relentlessly* – but symphs had no *skills*. They were just dive-bombing parasites with renegade feces. But quichyrds, on the other hand…

He breathed deeply, turned the dial, and winced as he thrust himself back, rolling onto his duff down the carved dirt steps to avoid potential dangers.

But instead…

Click, click, click. The dials spun wild, and the second lock squealed open. Twitch grinned, his fur still emitting wisps of smoke.

He stared up at the final riddle, perplexed. He read it aloud, cocking an eyebrow. "*Rich eaflics want it, poor wyls have it, semdrogs will concede it.*" He took a deep drag of air in and sighed. He didn't have a clue what it meant.

Outside his bulbous end of the tunnel, down the archaic stairway, Quistix strapped the last of the fortified armor on. She didn't wince at the skeletal form she had to mangle to get the pieces out.

Once the complete set of flawless armor was on, she felt like a new woman, energy restored. She was enraptured. She felt… alive.

"A little help up here!" Twitch sounded worried.

Quistix made her way up the stairs, metal armor pieces clattering together, bounding up steps with spritely energy - three at a time in her new enchanted boot-shields - until she was standing beside Twitch. She stared down at his singed fur, and he blinked hard and shook his head. "Don't ask."

"I won't." She scrunched her face and looked around.

"The armor looks good on you."

"Thank you."

"It hugs your curves."

"Of course you'd say that." She rolled her eyes. Eyes that had returned to their normal fresh-citrus coloring.

"This lock is tied to the riddles. I got the first and second ones correct, though the consequences for being wrong are quite unpleasant." He pointed at the third riddle etched above their heads. *"Rich eaflics want it, poor wyls have it, semdrogs will concede it."*

"That doesn't even make sense." She looked at the dials, "it has to be a species?"

"What do rich eaflics want?"

"Other eaflics?"

Twitch frowned. "When have you ever seen an eaflic with another eaflic?"

"Poor wyls have it."

"I've seen poor wyls with every type. Unlike everyone else in Destoria, we don't discriminate." He said it in a haughty tone.

"That's the truth. You guys will try to get lucky with everything."

"I take offense to that." Twitch squinted his eyes at her, annoyed.

"Semdrogs will concede it?"

"Not a frigging thing. When have you ever seen a semdrog concede to anything? They never think they're wrong."

"That's it!" Quistix flashed an almost alarmingly huge smile. Twitch had never seen her smile to that extent. It was like the suit of armor was making her manic. "Semdrogs will concede to nothing. Rich eaflics need nothing. Poor wyls…"

She faded off, realizing that that didn't quite solve the riddle as the last dial only held species. She stared at it for a moment and then grasped the central crank of the dial.

"Easy, Q. This chamber bites back. Don't spin it unless you know what you're doing." He crept backward toward the stairwell, clearing the holes where fire and arrows had ejected before.

"Here goes nothing." She cranked the dial, stopping where the notch pointed into the empty gap between the eaflic and wyl.

Click, click, click.

The dials whizzed in rapid circles over and over until the ground beneath her shook. She looked back at Twitch, worried. But he was halfway down the stairs in an act of self-preservation.

CLICK!

The last lock slid open, and light beamed through the slowly opening door. The rumbling slowed to a stop. They were in. They were staring into the bowels of the Ruby Palace dungeon.

Quistix's manic smile faded in a flash.

A horde of crimson soul reapers stared at her, their ghostly jaws dripping with slime, garnet eyes glimmering at the prospect of food. It was abundantly clear that they were voracious and hungry. And *pain* was on the menu.

50

The Grand Hall,
The Ruby Castle,
Desdemona,
Willowdale

Frok and Dally fluttered around the door, searching for metal pins to remove and slits they could wiggle through. Ralmeath tore violently at the door with her claws. They blunted against the reinforced metal bars of the towering front doors.

"You two, get down here. Rally, you're dulling your daggers. You can't get through that way," Kaem growled. "Stop and think for a second."

Ralmeath let out a series of groans, glancing around for a solution. Frok And Dally buzzed to Ralmeath's shoulders and stared at the door.

"There has to be a lever or a switch. Or… is this mammoth hunk a' wood completely barricaded?" Kaem questioned.

A loud *thwack* sounded behind the door as it shook.

They bolted away from the jostling door. Kaem readied her whip as Ralmeath protracted her claws. Dally and Frok swallowed gulps of air, readying their burps. Behind the thick, reinforced door arose the faint remnants of the voice beyond it.

"Come on, you!" It was a male, one familiar to Kaem.

Thwack! Thwack!

There was a long pause. Then, a final, resounding *thwack!*

Suddenly, the doors burst open. The splintered wood bracer cracked in half, revealing a set of curled akaih ram horns behind it. Arias tossed a single-sided wood-chopping ax to the ground with an echoing clank. He bent at the waist to catch his breath. "Those bars are tougher'n they *look*."

"That's why I have one of *these*." Kaem pointed to Ralmeath. Frok and Dally exhaled.

Arias laughed at the cheeky joke and stood up straight. Kaem emitted a sharp bird-like whistle of admiration, wowed by the castle's grand hall behind him. Exquisitely carved stone pillars spiraled toward the heavens, stopping at a large domed ceiling. The roof around it was muraled with images of Destorian soldiers waging an epic war with one another. The walls around them had been decorated with fading images of townsfolk cowering in terror at the scene above.

"Woah," Frok gushed, gripping the hair of Ralmeath's cheek for balance as she gazed up at the stunning artwork.

"Wealth is truly wasted on the rich." Kaem huffed, glancing in awe at the intricate artwork before refocusing on the task at hand.

Arias swiveled his head around in search of a threat, ever at the ready.

"It's so good to see you." A warm, friendly smile spread across her beak.

"You too, my friend."

"Okay," Kaem stepped through the massive doors over a hill of shattered beams, "let's do this."

Arias nodded, gesturing for them to follow. He darted down a nearby hallway. Kaem followed closely behind. Ralmeath seemed dazzled by the depiction of the fiery fray above. The lofty corridor glimmered in a rainbow of colors, all projections from colorful stained-glass fractals from the numerous, massive windows, many of which depicted scenes of Destorian species bowing before the ruby crown.

At the end of the hall, Arias pressed open the hefty wooden door and peered in. As soon as he saw the coast was clear, he waved the others in. They wove through long donik tables in the neat rows of the soldier's mess hall, gathering near the door on the opposing side. He pulled the handle and cracked it open, jolting at the surprise.

He was face-to-face with one of his guards.

"Urwin," Arias addressed his subordinate with a familiar tone and straightened his posture. "These are friends to the cause."

"Understood, sir," Urwin's tone was ultra-serious.

"Why aren't you with the others," Arias asked. "Today is not your day for battle."

"She ordered me to stay on duty and fetch a pitcher of wine for her nerves. Hasn't let me out of her sight all day. I'm heading that way now."

"Where is she?" Arias asked.

"In her chambers, sir." Urwin's eyes darted toward the floor.

"Spilled blood has no loyalty. Hurry. Get to safety immediately." Arias slapped him on the back and waved for the others to follow the akaih toward the chambers.

Urwin nodded to Arias and then double-timed his steps toward the entrance from which they had just come.

Kaem, Ralmeath, Arias, and the pleoms wound through the twisted corridors and climbed up a set of stairs beneath a glass window depicting Willowdale's symbolic tree in the town center decades before.

Arias counted the doors until he arrived at the fourth on the right. Without warning, he threw it open.

Exos screeched, then sighed when she realized who it was. "Arias! Why would you barge in like that?!" She tugged at the strings of the corset at the front of her dress and tied them. The billowing fabric of her scarlet sleeves swished as she pulled the knot tight. Her once sensual, soothing voice had now morphed into a sharp, indignant tone. "Where are the men? I looked outside my door, but no one was stationed there. Even the damn chambermaid is nowhere to be found! What is going on in this castle? A *mutiny?*" She chuckled at the absurdity of her words.

They wouldn't dare.

She spotted the quichyrd as she brushed past Arias. Ralmeath crouched beneath the door frame and stood up inside. The great chamber suddenly felt small with the Bramolt bear in it, like the cramped cage of a feral animal.

"Who are you?"

The three of them stared back at Exos. The barbed whip unfurled from Kaem's claw.

"Guards!" Exos shouted toward the hallway. No response. No hurried footsteps, no clattering armor. *Only silent betrayal.*

"I don't hear them coming. Do *you?*" Arias crossed his hairy arms.

Black smoke tendrils wisped out of Exos' palms. "*What did you do?*"

"As head of the royal guard, aptly appointed by *you*, it's my duty to defend Destoria from those who seek to destroy it. Even if the threat itself is someone who sits on its throne."

Exos nodded and laughed, her mind whirling. "*Treason*, Arias? Maybe you *do* have a spine after all." She slipped on her silken flats. "But this was not well-planned. Your men are not the only people who will fight for their Queen. You'll have to gut those you swore to protect. There are monsters in my dungeon, all hungry and eager to be unleashed. Are you ready for innocent blood on those spotless hands of yours?"

"No innocent blood will be shed. This ends here and now." He drew his sword from his sheath and pointed it at her.

Ralmeath protracted her claw, and Kaem reeled back her barbed whip. Frok and Dally nodded to each other beneath Ralmeath's snout and breathed in deeply again.

Exos stood unmoving, with a broad grin cast across her crimson lips. "Three misfits and two little rats want to battle the Queen of the Isle? *Let's have it.* It's been ages since I've had a good fight. "

Kaem whipped, lashing the leather and barbs around Exos' wrist. She tugged hard, tearing at the flesh of her forearm. Exos screamed out, swaying to dodge Frok and Dally as they swarmed around her like a whizzing swarm of angry, fire-burping bees.

Exos stretched her hand out toward Kaem and clasped her fist shut. With a sickening crunch, Kaem's legs twisted and buckled. The quichyrd screamed out in pain as she crumpled to the floor, grasping her mangled limbs.

Exos plucked the barbs from her skin, dropping the bloodied weapon to the floor. Ralmeath's soulful, brown eyes darkened, and she sprinted toward the pale Queen on all fours. Exos reached out and focused her magic to lift the huge bear off the floor, slinging her enormous body toward the ceiling. Despite her swatting and kicking, Ralmeath was stuck steadfastly to the roof by wispy, octopus-like tentacles of black magic. More tentacles reached out, snatching Frok and Dally, hurling them out of the windows behind her. The glass exploded. Dally and Frok screeched as they slammed against the opposite walls of the U-shaped ruby palace.

With the others dispatched, Exos stepped toward Arias. Thinking fast, Arias raised his hardened blade and buried the tip into the center of her chest. She winced and tensed her jaw from the pain. The sting of it ignited the bottomless pit of rage inside her.

"We could have been something beautiful," she said wistfully. "Goodbye, Arias," Exos lifted her hands toward him.

A crushing pressure grew within his rib cage. Thundering erratically, his heart thudded out of rhythm under an invisible strain. His breathing turned to raspy gasps. He dropped his long sword and clutched his chest. Within a few seconds, the familiar beat was silenced. As his vision faded, she hurled his body through the window with her dark force, shattering the ornate glass depiction.

"No!" Kaem squawked, unable to stop her from the act of cruelty.

The throw sent his hairy, armored body tumbling into the courtyard, smashing down onto his curled horns with a sickening crunch of bone and meat on rock. The fall was great, and the akaih died on impact. The Queen stared out the shattered window at his lifeless body and swallowed hard.

"Traitorous *coward*." Her lip quivered. She bit down harshly to make it stop.

Kaem mustered her strength and lashed her whip from the floor, wrapping it around Exos' neck. Distracted by searing pain, the Queen lost focus and Rally crashed down from the vaulted ceiling, cracking the stone floor beneath her. Exos gasped as metal bits tore at the tender flesh of her throat, tightening with her struggle. Her frantic fingertips tore at the leather braid, fighting to tug it free. Green-tinged blood trickled down porcelain flesh as Kaem tugged her backward, slamming her to the floor. The cracks spread further, separating into a sizable fissure. The separation of the sides of the crevasse sent fractured pebbles tumbling into the mess hall below them.

Exos gargled a scream, trying to use her magic to escape. She couldn't concentrate as she fought for air. Kaem jerked harder on the whip. The metal dug into Exo's windpipe as a wet whistle screeched out. Exos snatched Arias' abandoned long sword, grasping the handle. She swung it clumsily over her head with a bit of luck, slicing the braided leather straps in half, freeing herself.

With all the commotion and Ralmeath scrambling to right herself, more of the floor crumbled beneath them, sending them all tumbling with hunks of stone floor to the level below. Kaem and Ralmeath crashed into one of the donik wood tables, smashing it to pieces. Exos crashed into a table beside them, tipping it sideways with the force, and rolled to the floor. She hungrily sucked in air, peering at her foes from between the bench and the table.

Ralmeath sat up and looked at Kaem, who cawed weakly.

Exos peered up at the fractured, looming, stony hunks of the floor above and summoned her magic to pull some free. As they broke loose, Rally threw herself on top of Kaem, covering the warrior in the nick of time. The gray slab crashed down on Rally's back.

Exos waited, watching for movement. The hunk of stone remained unmoving.

Satisfied, Exos pulled herself to her feet. She clutched at the wounds in her throat, dribbling blood down her chest, staining the crimson cloth at her breasts. She gurgled and wheezed as she walked down the corridor to the far exit, toward the dungeon.

As the door groaned shut behind her, the pile of rock jostled.

BRRRRAAAAAAAAAH!

Ralmeath strained and roared, struggling to press the slab away and free them. As she shifted it aside, she peered down at Kaem, legs twisted and mangled. Frok and Dally looked down through the collapsed floor, a few scratches on their bellies and cheeks, but otherwise unscathed.

Ralmeath knelt beside Kaem and let out a sad roar. She dug her claws into Kaem's hip pocket and tugged out Aurora's prong. She held the tiny piece of antler, dwarfed by her massive paws, and snapped it in half. She rubbed the two edges together, dusting Kaem with its healing powder.

"Wow," Kaem coughed, scrunching her face as she jerked her legs back into place. "What a bitch."

51

*The Dungeon of the Ruby Palace,
Desdemona,
Willowdale*

Quistix stared into the blazing red eyes of a crimson soul reaper and fired an ice bolt out of pure, frightened reflex. The icicle went awry, missing and bouncing off the tunnel of gray stone behind, then shattering like glass into a million pieces on the floor. The reaper grinned a ghastly smile full of teeth, an expression of pleasure that looked more like a hideous grimace.

The insidious specter attacked her, knocking her backward and down the dirt steps toward

Hadina's tomb, bowling over Twitch in the process. He protracted his pointed claws and carved into the reaper in a fast flurry of movement, shredding its rotten, undead flesh like a tiger. The reaper roared in pain at the fierce efforts of the wyl. While its mouth hung open, the ear-piercing scream reversed, sucking Quistix toward itself with mighty force. She howled in pain.

Twitch struck again with a barrage of vicious slices, and the graying, rotten organs of the creature fell out into a repulsive, wet mess of rancid viscera and acidic bile. The reaper went limp, draping itself over the pile of its own innards.

Quistix flashed Twitch a satisfied half-smile over the corpse. "Nice work!"

"I know." Twitch grinned, cocky. The fur of his face was flecked with dark blood.

She high-fived him, out of breath, and winced as his paw-like hand connected with hers in a rank slap that left her already grimy, elven hand coated in coagulating fluid.

"One down." He wiped his paws on his tattered pants and withdrew his bow.

The duo stepped over the revolting corpse and headed up the staircase to the narrow catacombs. She had to squeeze through where the walls narrowed severely, scraping her metal breastplates and backplates against the walls. Her heart pounded in her chest, and she was thankful that Aurora had agreed to wait outside. They crept up the long stairway; her thoughts drifted to Kaem, Ralmeath, and Frok. She wondered how they fared on their end.

But she wouldn't have to wonder for long.

ROOOOOOAAAAAHHHHHHHH! Ralmeath's voice growled viciously, forcing a smile onto Quistix's face. It sounded like a groaning boulder shuffling against something rough, vibrating the floor beneath her metal greaves with its powerful bass.

Twitch clutched the stone wall beside him, pressing his back against it, breathing hard.

"You okay?" She looked concerned.

"Yeah. Rally's just... *really* damned scary when she's angry." He gulped and turned back toward the light at the top of the staircase. He readied his bow and bolted up the steps two at a time, listening to violent squawks and the clinking of what had to be bear claws swiping at stone.

Quistix pulled *Swordbreaker* out of her leather strap, readying herself. Its minimal weight felt impossibly heavy. Though the suit of armor she wore was lightweight, made of some sort of metal she'd never seen before in all her years of smithing. It wasn't the sort of heft she was used to carrying around with her weapons. Between all of the magic drained by Hadina, the force of the weight, and the physical exertion from battling the witch, the elven mage was exhausted. It worried her to go into battle again, so deeply drained.

BRAAAAAAAAHHHH!

Quistix heard another roar as she burst through the staircase behind a short wall of crates at the mouth of the dungeon. They hunched down, barely allowing the tops of their heads to be exposed as they surveyed the area. The oblong room was vast, stretching over fifty feet long and nearly twenty feet wide, with rounded edges like an egg funneling toward an open door on the other side. Beyond it sat a mountainous pile of stony rubble. *The topside entrance,* Quistix thought. The rectangle of light showed a mess hall with a palace exit at the far end.

Between the walls of drug-filled crates was a mob of undead beings perilously enclosing Ralmeath. Two-headed tailed infernals hissed and snarled, waiting to taste fresh blood. Two malevolent crimson soul reapers watched and screeched wraith-like, their red eyes aglow.

The room's edges were cluttered with stacked crates labeled *DIKEEKA* in stenciled letters on the diagonal wooden supports, just like the ones they'd seen on the ship ride from Evolt.

"This must be where Exos is stashing her supply. She's withholding from Destorians. She is probably trying to get people hooked to choke out the supply and take over as the primary dealer. She wants a monopoly on the stuff. Once people get hooked, they'll pay *any* price for this poison," Twitch whispered.

Suddenly, a round circle of neon light and platinum sparks illuminated on the left dungeon wall, momentarily halting their efforts. The spinning circle turned black in the center, and the blinding light and colors around it intensified. The opening turned glassy, like a jet-black scrying mirror, and then spun out like the blades of a camera aperture, creating a tunnel through the center.

Tar-black feathers with green opalescent tips came out first, gripping the bright sides of the circle in the stone, pulling the body of the quichyrd attached to it out through the portal hole.

"What the…?" Quistix could hear Kaem say from across the stone-laden expanse.

As the ancient quichyrd birthed through the tunnel, she smiled. The reptilian scales of her face looked wrinkled from the ravages of time beneath feathers jutting out from her various features. Her lime-green eyes shone like twin beacons through the dungeon, only illuminated by dim, everlasting torch-sconces every few feet.

"Ceosteol," Twitch whispered to the slack-jawed warrior beside him, "creator of the undead." He stared at Quistix for a moment as she crouched beside him in awe of the spectacle. It was easy for him to forget that just a few months ago, she'd been a simple blacksmith, single mother on a grassy little hilltop in Bellaneau, never having seen a fraction of the wonders and nightmares of Destoria.

"There you are, you haggard, old *turkey*! You can't *do* this," Kaem shouted, growling as she limped painfully behind a dikeeka crate. "We won't let you ravage our land with your little *playthings*," she squawked from the far end of the left wall.

Ralmeath's guttural roar arose from the center of a horde of reapers. She gnashed her jaws.

Kaem tied the two, severed hunks of her whip together with an ugly knot. Ceosteol lifted a hand to cast a spell, and Kaem snapped it hard at the old woman. The stinging end caught tightly on her outstretched winged arm, bloodying her immediately. Oddly, the quichyrds looked similar, save for the tattered orphan rags Ceosteol donned and her moss-green, glowing eyes. Kaem looked like a more youthful sibling to the ancient quichyrd, scarred and battle-worn but still cunning and clever.

Her steel-plated leather armor was covered in black slime, the same substance leaking from the pile of shredded black-eyed beings lying still in pieces near the crate. Ralmeath had done a number on the tar-eyed monstrosities. They now looked like a lump of gangrenous pulled pork with hunks of scalp and strewn facial features hidden in the mess.

The vine beneath Quistix's boot began to writhe and squirm like a snake suddenly alive.

"Uh, Q, what the–"

Twitch was interrupted by a thick vine wrapping his snout tightly, clamping his jaws shut. She inspected the ground beneath their feet and saw a web of brown foliage creeping quickly, wrapping up their legs, slithering around their extremities like a boa constrictor.

Quistix hollered a war cry and slammed the blade of her two-headed ax down, severing some of the vines. She swiped down again and again, hacking the foliage into pieces. It had taken hold of Twitch, raising him off the ground and over the crates in staccato movements - up and down. The vines heaved him into full view of the nefarious horde before them. His muffled grunts and wiggles were useless.

"Hold on, Twitch!" Quistix chopped at the thick, trunk-like base of the roots holding the wyl in the air, gnawing pieces out with every slash.

"There you is, Quizzy!" Frok's tiny voice bounced off the walls through the dank dungeon air before she turned back to Ceosteol and belched fire into the old quichyrd's face. The plumage singed off, leaving Ceosteol's scaly skin bald, stripped of her chest and face feathers. She patted out the fire on her ruined clothing with a clawed hand, but it was too late. The filthy bits of fabric and feathers fell to the floor in burned patches.

"*Nova vestimenta sua!*" She chanted the words, embarrassed. A new, drab garb appeared, modestly covering her sad, naked form once again.

Quistix stopped mid-hack and nearly dropped *Swordbreaker* to the ground when she saw the source of her misery. *She should have known…*

It was *Exos*, slumped in the moat between the right wall and a mound of double-stacked dikeeka crates, obscuring her from the throng of monstrosities. Toxic-looking fluid dribbled out of the wounds on her throat in rivulets, down her heaving breasts.

Exos glared in her direction, wounded and exhausted. The vines pulsed with her ragged breathing. Even from afar, Quistix could hear her gurgle from her injury. Yet, somehow, even in hiding, at a fraction of her strength, the witch who had been hunting her for months was still so powerful. Enough so that Twitch was hoisted high overhead, clawing desperately at the vine constricting his torso.

Ceosteol screamed from the opposite side of the room, past the beasts. "*Plumis novis!*" She tightened her claws as if she were having a stroke. Suddenly, new green-tipped black feathers sprouted between her hideous, lizard-like scales.

Frok and Dally fluttered together and hosed down a growling tailed infernal with a burst of flames from their tiny mouths. It yipped with both snarling snouts, shrieking in echoing pain. It skittered clumsily away, lighting up the crimson reaper beside it. The pleoms high-fived in the air, clamping their tiny claws together.

"We's make a great team," Dally shouted.

"I wish 'Rora coulda seen dat!" Frok giggled.

RAAAAAAAAAA! Ralmeath roared to try to warn her of the dangers behind her. Ceosteol stretched her claws straight out and shot an icicle at Frok, missing the dragonling by an inch.

Seeing her family in harm's way sent Quistix into a boiling rage, giving her a second wind of adrenaline. She wouldn't let them down like Danson.

She *couldn't*.

Thinking fast, Quistix knew from her recent run-in with Hadina that she had better accuracy shooting ice bolts as fire was erratic and uncontrollable. She conjured a large icicle in her mind, concentrating hard on it brewing within her. Her eyes turned white as clouds, and she growled. Her arm sprung toward Exos, and the bolt knocked the raven-haired witch backward, spearing her through the shoulder. Her body shot into a square wooden crate, shattering the glass vials inside.

Twitch was dropped to the ground. He tumbled, gasping, quickly wriggling free of the thick vines wound around his form. Hidden behind a small stack of crates, Ceosteol possessed one of her snarling infernals. She watched through both sets of its eyes as it leaped at Twitch, soon startled when it was halted in mid-air. Ralmeath had snatched it, gripping both of its heads away from her body, far enough to be out of striking distance of its tail. With a forceful tug, she tore the infernal apart. She hurled the two incapacitated halves toward the wall, rendering them useless. Ceosteol redirected her focus and possessed another.

Twitch grasped at his throat and gave a nod of appreciation to Ralmeath, then retrieved what was left of his bow. The vines had crushed it. Now, nothing but useless twine and splintered wood.

"Uh, Quistix?!" Twitch yelled out. She turned toward him, noticing the broken bow resting in his quivering hands.

Quistix recalled one of the spells Professor Glenshire taught her in Apex, and she struggled to cast it.

"*Ligwam restituet*," she called, pointing a finger at his weapon.

Nothing happened.

"Was something supposed to…?" Twitch seemed confused.

"*Dammit*," Quistix groaned.

Ralmeath snatched up one of the infernals by anything she could grasp, wrapping her second hand around its snake tail and jerking it from the rest of the infernal's body. The undead hounds shrieked in pain as she whipped the snake tail harshly to kill it. She hurled the rest of the body into the others, knocking over two more as it grabbed the next to dispatch.

Kaem wrapped the length of her whip around her hand to adjust for the close quarters as she put the rest of the group to work. "Quistix, gimme your axe!" Kaem shouted to her.

Focusing all of her attention on magic, Quistix tugged the twisted handle of *Swordbreaker* from her belt strap. She tossed it over the snarling teeth and hissing tails to Kaem, who snatched it from the air by the twisted metal handle. Kaem lashed gnashing jaws closed with her whip. She then stepped on the strap between them, pinning the infernals' heads to the floor as she slammed Swordbreaker down on the first head, then the second, dodging and slashing at their venomous tails until the three-headed beasts were completely incapacitated.

The room was now in utter pandemonium.

Watching her babies fall was too much for Ceosteol to bear. She decided on a different target. In the back, an infernal snapped both sets of jaws, jumping awkwardly on its hind legs and springing into the air to snatch Frok. Its teeth clacked together with a hard, wet smack, gnashing violently at the pleoms. Frok erupted in a scared cry, buzzing away from the beast. Ceosteol shot her own wide blast of ice through the air, bringing Frok and Dally down behind some crates. The undead hounds chased them through the wooden maze-like hunting dogs.

"*Lignum restituet!*" This time, the chant worked, restoring Twitch's bow into a single piece again, right before his eyes.

"Yes!" No matter how many times he'd seen the elf perform magic, he didn't think he'd ever be able to get used to it.

Snapping jaws, slashing claws, swiping blades, and loosed arrows whizzed across each other. Deafening cracks of Kaem's whip and thunderous booms resonated as skeletal bodies were slung against the wall. Above the noise, the pleoms' shrill cries rang out.

Quistix screamed, "I'm coming, Frok!"

As she climbed over the crates and leaped onto the ones near Frok, Exos staggered to her feet. Fluid rushed from her new injuries in gory spurts. Twitch loaded an arrow and fired one into her lower back, piercing it cleanly and plunging it straight through her chest.

Exos turned to look at him. She was in terrible shape. He aimed again and fired another, but she caught the arrow mid-air with a shocking display of precision. His jaw slung open in astonishment at the speed at which one would have to move to accomplish such a feat. She snapped the arrow in half with her powerful fingers. Blood dripped from her grinning, red lips. She tossed it to the floor and ripped out the one hanging from her stomach, wincing in pain. She staggered toward him, pointing with it. There was a chunk of meat – *her meat* – still stuck to the tip.

"I am going to enjoy this." She laughed. But the laugh turned into a cough, spattering more blood from her mouth than she ever had when she was alive.

Frok and Dally launched into the air to avoid the snarling double-headed creation beneath them. Ceosteol cast another spell. *Lightning*. A blinding, jagged bolt of electricity snapped out into the air like a white jellyfish tendril. It snapped right between them and sent the pleoms fluttering in different directions.

To the right, Quistix saw Exos facing off with Twitch. She snuck up behind the wounded Queen and kicked Exos in the back of the knee, toppling her like a tree. As she dropped, the armor-clad warrior grabbed a handful of Exos' black hair and slammed her head into the rock wall before tossing her bleeding body to the ground.

Twitch raced over to Frok and Dally, and Kaem weakly whistled. He looked up, and the quichyrd tossed him a small single-sided ax from one of the loops on her weapon belt. He caught it in the air and whipped around, hacking at the heads of the hungry zombified dogs with the weapon. The pleom cries rose from beneath the vicious snarls as he slashed the beasts without prejudice.

As Exos struggled to rise, she muttered, "This... isn't like the fables... where we fight as equals. This," she coughed, struggling with every word like a chore, "is the story where... I squash you like the bug you are." She spat up more ruby sputum, "because I *can*. Because I *want* to." In a flash, she summoned a jagged piece of dikeeka bottle from the floor and slashed at her elven adversary. It glanced off Quistix's metal chest plate. She kicked Exos' wrist to disarm her. The shard flew in the air and astonishingly seated itself back in Exos' palm as if tethered with a springy, elastic cord.

Even wounded, Exos was powerful.

Exos stabbed the unprotected seam between Quistix's front and rear leg plates, tearing through the flesh of her right thigh. Quistix yowled and clutched her injured leg.

Exos smirked; after months of hunting the elf and tearing her life apart bit by bit, she was excited to wound her *personally* for once.

Grrrrrrrrlllllllllaaaaaaaawwwww!

A growl sounded. Quistix craned her neck to see a tailed infernal behind her, licking both of its mouths simultaneously. The undead thing snarled and exposed both sets of its decaying teeth in a warning.

"Q, look out!" Kaem squawked from atop a dikeeka box in the corner, grinding her own point from Aurora's antlers into dust. Without the use of both legs, extraction would be exponentially harder.

Three decomposing creatures fanned out around Quistix, and she backed up against a wall, readying for an attack. But the infernals walked past, their evil green sights locked on their *true* target:

Exos.

They swarmed the Queen like a troop of loyal, glowy-eyed servants. Their elongated toenails clicked against the rough stone surface of the dungeon. Snake tails rattled, ready to strike. One howled like a wolf, hungry for blood, waiting patiently for the word from their green-eyed master.

They hungered for violence.

"What is this?" Exos laughed at Ceosteol. "I thought we were in this together?"

With that, Ceosteol buckled with laughter, nearly falling down on the stone floor. She had to catch herself against the wall near the still-sparking portal. "You can't be serious." She finally managed to regain her composure. "You have used me in every way I can imagine throughout the years. Everything you are is thanks to me. And for that, I'm ashamed of myself. Of all the monsters I have created, *you* are by far the worst. You petulant, entitled, spoiled little *wretch*. You hung a carrot in front of my face for decades because of my babies." She smiled down at one of the infernals, and it looked up at her, wagging its rattlesnake tail like a happy pup. "Maybe because you wouldn't know what loyalty even looks like. Maybe because you don't know the value of *obedience*. The joy of *creation*..." The quichyrd's neon eyes glowed brightly. She looked overtaken by madness. "It's time for that to end. It's time to do what I should have done when you were just a *sadistic* little girl!"

Exos glanced around, arms out defensively, as she tried to keep all of the monsters in her sight. "Look—"

Ceosteol cut her off with a booming screech. "*Impetum! Infantes meos!*"

That was their cue.

Exos was tackled and thrown backward by a vicious infernal. She landed hard with a force that knocked the air out of her already weak lungs. She pushed herself up on trembling hands only to find she was face-to-*faces* with a mange-ridden, double-headed infernal. Its breath reeked of decomposition. Its skin stunk like *rot*. Horrid-smelling bile dripped from its fangs in ice-cold globs. Ichor and pus oozed from open sores where its exposed rib cage shone through patches of missing fur.

Exos tried to stand, but in a flash, she felt its chilled claws slice into her shoulders, shredding her pallid flesh as it climbed her like a mountain. Another jabbed its hefty paws into her, slamming her against the stone wall beneath an ever-burning sconce. Another raged against her slender legs, snapping into the bones beneath with noxious, plaque-covered teeth.

"Ceosteol, get these wretched things off me!"

"It's finally over, Exos… for the both of us." She savored the surge of power, hands quivering with adrenaline.

"Just, please, *reconsider*," Exos pleaded, her voice no longer sounding like her own.

"In my years of servitude, I've considered *and reconsidered* this *thousands* of times." The cosmos whirled in Ceosteol's nuclear eyes, illuminating her harsh birdlike features with a galactic glow. "I'm just sad I only get to experience it once." She cackled and then screamed, "*gutture!*"

Another infernal leapt onto Exos. Its chilling drool slapped across her face just before it locked its strong jaws onto her oozing, wounded throat.

And then it shook.

All three beasts latched on, their teeth ripping right through her flesh. She tried to speak, tried to scream for help, but the seizing pressure clamped around her neck allowed nothing more than wet coughs and bloody gurgles to escape. Blood poured from the punctures, dousing Exos' in a waterfall of her own vibrant post-life force.

She tumbled to the floor. An overwhelming sense of dread and paralyzing fear washed over her as her breaths escaped through the new, gaping holes. A metallic taste filled her mouth. Her lungs failed to muster even the weakest of screams, and her sight narrowed, then blackened before her vision failed completely. Exos convulsed violently on the floor. Her head sounded several sickening cracks against the stone.

She lay near the spot where she had tortured Hadina all those years ago. As she drifted into the Ether, she heard her mother's voice:

"*Darkness has come,*" it cooed.

While Ceosteol was enraptured by the carnage and death of the Queen before her unnatural eyes,

Ralmeath attacked the quichyrd, bowling her frail, old body into a wall of wooden crates, smashing their planks and the glass contents inside. The force of the smash instantly coated both of them with black, opalescent liquid. Ralmeath raised a paw to swipe at the old woman's face, but her neon eyes connected with Ralmeath's, and she cast a windblast spell, blowing the snow-white Bramolt bear backward into more boxes.

Excited by Ralmeath's cries, a crimson soul reaper sprung to life and wrapped its ghastly skeletal arms around Twitch. It erupted in a reverse scream, inflicting excruciating pain on the wyl. Frok and Dally, worse for the wear after their infernal attack, came fluttering to his aid, throwing hunks of broken glass and wood at the creature, knowing their fiery belches would do harm to the wyl at such close proximity.

"Kaem! *Swordbreaker!* Give it here!" Kaem looked at the axe and knew what she meant. Grabbing ahold of the bloodied blade, she tossed the handle toward Quistix.

Quistix snatched *Swordbreaker* from the air and readied herself to take a shot at it, wrapping her hands around the bloodied fabric from her son's shirt that still hung from the handle. The closeness made her wild magic too unpredictable, and she'd never forgive herself if she hurt Twitch.

The infernals skittered away from the foul, black solution puddled around Ceosteol and huddled in the far corner near the doorway to the upper palace. The intoxicating liquor glugged out of sealed containers, filling in the cracks and crevices between the stones on the cobbled floor. Ceosteol's mossy eyes shot open, realizing how much of it she was soaked in. She created the drug many years ago – much by accident – and knew too well just how flammable the solution was.

"Hey, you!" Dally's squeaky voice shouted at the soul reaper as he lugged a broken wooden slat at its head. "Let Twitch go, you big, ugly dum-dum!"

As the board smacked the red-eyed apparition in the forehead, it dropped the wyl and stretched its ghoulish arm a freakish distance, snatching the pleom right out of the air and tossing him into his mouth like a wad of chewing gum. Twitch hurtled at the specter as the reaper gnashed the dragonling with its sharp fangs.

"Dally!" Frok shrieked and blasted its garnet eyes with a burp of fire, and the reaper dropped its living chew-toy. The reaper breathed in, sucking in the excruciating cries of the dragonling at its feet, feeding on his pain. Twitch dove to grab Dally from the ground and took off running behind the last few still-in-tact crates.

Dally was in bad shape, poked full of holes, his lungs gasping for air that wouldn't come. Twitch clutched him tightly, eyes wildly searching his mangled little body. He pulled his portion of esteg-antler out of his pocket with a trembling hand just as he was tackled by the reaper. The force of the hit tossed the bit of horn into the darkened hole of the portal, and it disappeared into the abyss.

"No!"

Quistix and Ralmeath worked in tandem to attack the reaper. The bear wrestled him to the ground, and Quistix raised *Swordbreaker* high overhead and brought it down on the reaper's neck, severing his head from his body in one clean swipe that sent a shockwave of reverberation up through her armored arms.

"Where's your horn? Dally...he's..." Twitch cried, "It's bad."

"I ground it up already! Down in the tomb, remember?" She looked at the dragonling. "Stay with us, Dally!"

"I just used all of mine, too," Kaem squawked from the corner, hoisting herself up to her feet and hobbling forward, whip at the ready, eyes locked on Ceosteol. Frok began to wail loudly, causing the reapers to grin at the sadistic fuel.

"We have to get him out of here! We have to get him to Aurora. She's holding the rest of the antler for us." Quistix felt helpless at the sight of the injured pleom. She aimed her palms at Ceosteol, shooting large shards of ice. The old quichyrd ducked, scurrying out of the way just as the frost bolts slammed into the stone where she'd just been.

She shot one back at Quistix, hitting her square in the chest. It glanced off the magically-fortified armor, and the quichyrd fired another, this time burrowing it powerfully between the metal plates of her armor, jolting her electrically with unrelenting magical force.

"You's hurt my Dally! You's *not* gonna hurt my Quizzy," Frok screamed, tears in her eyes. She pinned her wings to her side and shot down like an arrow at the quichyrd. She sucked air in and burped loudly, blasting Ceosteol's face with flames, scorching the old mage's feathery body.

Infuriated, the crone batted the flames and thrust an open hand at Frok. From it, she materialized a molten, metal arrow and fired it mercilessly at the pleom, catching Frok square in the chest. The brutal collision sent her tiny, bulbous body whirling into the unforgiving stone wall with a heavy *wham*! Her tiny skull made hard contact, and she slid to the floor, face down. *Unmoving.*

Twitch raced toward the dragonling, scooping her up in his furry arms like a baby. She looked at him, dazed. She smiled. So did he. He was overwhelmed with relief. With a hit like that, she should have died.

And then she coughed.

Blood and spittle-flecked his fur-covered cheeks, and his smile faded instantly. Her tiny, gasping voice spoke, eyes huge and innocent.

"Will you tell 'Rora dat I love her?" Her voice was as sweet as sugarcane.

With tears flooding Twitch's eyes, he shook his head. "No. Tell her yourself. You hear me?"

"She was my best friend in the whole world." Her voice sounded so happy. As if she were in another world, one full of peace instead of the dungeon battlefield filled with drugs and turmoil. "Tell her... she made my whole life."

With that, she relaxed. Her body hung limp in his arms.

Lifeless and still.

Quistix threw her head back, eyes white with fury.

Ceosteol's eyes widened to the size of crabapples. She had to get out. *Fast.*

The elf exploded into a scream, releasing a shockwave of white-hot fire that flooded the dungeon and belched down the narrow catacomb hallways toward Hadina's tomb. Kaem, Twitch, and Ralmeath barely had enough time to duck below crates. Twitch pressed himself against the back of the elf's armor as the heat singed his remaining hair.

It was too late.

The fireball smashed into the wall with a loud woof, igniting the dikeeka spilled in the grooves of the floor in an instant.

With the whoosh of her black wings to aid her, Ceosteol launched herself through the portal from which she'd come, narrowly escaping the flaming blast. Kaem bolted toward her, momentarily unafraid of the portal into the unknown, but she didn't make it in time. In just a fraction of a second, the portal sealed, the circle of sparks was squelched, and Kaem rammed head-first into the flaming rock wall. She bounced backward, rolling on the stone floor to make sure she wasn't on fire.

"We let her go!" Quistix screamed as a baffled look of confusion spread across her sooty face. The line of black oil around the room ignited into an oblong ring of fire. The combustible material turned the room into a smoky inferno in mere moments.

Quistix waved her hands in the air, sending a whirlwind of suspended ice through the valley of fire. A glass-like pathway was left in its wake, several feet in the air, melting rapidly over the flames below.

"Come on!" Quistix grabbed Frok out of Twitch's hands and broke into a dead run, charging over the ice, her path cracking as she crossed. She urged the others to follow suit as the remaining infernals snapped at her, clawing at the hovering, icy road from their spots on the floor.

Flames crept closer. One infernal whined, and another howled. They were more scared than angry now. Quistix felt a pang of guilt at their inescapable fate despite their noxious, undead existence.

A hunk of the path near the door cracked off and fell into a pooled puddle of the black liquid, splattering the last crimson soul reaper between her and the exit. He clasped his chest and face, his taut, gaunt skin bubbling beneath blistering black oil. He let out an ear-piercing scream, unlike anything they had ever heard before.

Quistix slid across the melting path. Her metal boot covers clacked against the ice like a scrambling horse. She felt the vibrations from Ralmeath and the others nipping closely at her heels.

With the blaze at their backs, the wounded band of misfits scurried onward through the mess hall, listening to the sound of the dogs yowling in pain behind them as the flames overtook the palace.

BOOM!

A crate of dikeeka exploded, shaking the stone floors below and above them. Huge hunks of the ceiling collapsed. The structural integrity of the palatial building had been compromised when Exos' chambers were destroyed, and now the upper floor began to follow suit, crumbling down like a deadly house of cards.

BOOM! BOOM!

Back-to-back combustions rang out. The dogs stopped howling. Kaem limped quickly, leading them out. Rally caught a falling hunk of the ceiling to the back, nearly crushing her to death, but she pressed the fallen slab off of her with all of her might and hobbled toward the front doors the late

Arias had bashed open. They skidded out into the courtyard, where several guards standing around Arias' tangled corpse saw them, staring with their steely eyes.

And then something miraculous happened.

One *kneeled.*

Then *another.*

Then the rest.

They took a reverent knee for the saviors of their cause.

BOOM!

The rumbling force of the biggest blast collapsed the second story of the castle completely, knocking the connected towers inward like leaning trees in a hurricane. The spires atop the tower engulfed slowly in a golden blaze, and fire spread up the mounded curtains and furniture trapped inside. As Quistix and the others limped deeper into the courtyard, away from the building, they heard the palace windows crack and shatter, wiping the visual history of Destoria into oblivion.

52

Cobblestone Courtyard,
The Ruby Palace, Desdemona,
Willowdale

"Set them down. Please, Frok, hold on," Aurora cried out as they gathered in the courtyard. Quistix set Frok and Dally's limp bodies on a patch of grass sprung between a crack in the cobblestones.

Never taking her eyes off Frok, Quistix stammered, struggling to find the words. "Give me that... the... the *prong*! The antler, give it to me!" Twitch reached into the pack, slung across Aurora's shoulder, and plucked out a shorn piece from Aurora's blown-off rack. Quistix snatched it and frantically scraped it against the stone beside the limp pleoms. A fine powder was released, leaving behind a small amount of neon dust.

"They're not breathing." Twitch's eyes welled up with tears. "By the Gods, *Frok*..."

Quistix snapped. "She just needs some air. Back up and let her breathe!" She pinched some dust with her fingertips and dabbed it on Frok's scaly lips. The neon hue loomed over the dragonling's mouth, never seeping into the skin. She did the same to Dally.

Neither moved.

Tears rolled down the sides of Aurora's furry face.

"Why isn't it working?" Quistix yelled in panic. "Come on! Work!" Her voice pitched with desperation.

"It's not working because... she's *gone*. They're dead." Aurora's voice cracked. She curled up in a tight ball and outstretched her neck, resting her head beside Frok. A silence fell among them. Quistix feared she was right.

"You can't leave me!" Aurora sobbed.

Quistix leaned back on her heels, eyes locked on Frok's lifeless body. "No. NO! She's not gone. She needs more." The elf feverishly scraped the horn-prong on the ground, the edges of her armor clattering together with every movement. Twitch grabbed her arm, but she yanked it away. She screamed, picking up more dust. She tipped Frok's lower jaw down and sprinkled it inside. Her tiny lips hung open.

"Come on, please!" Quistix begged. She felt like she was losing another child. She'd grown to love and protect Frok, as if she were kin, throughout their wild adventure.

Twitch turned away, unable to control the torrent of tears rushing to his eyes.

Quistix stared for a long moment, holding her breath and waiting for the healing to take hold. Frok's stab wound healed shut, and the mage gasped. "She's healing! Please! Come on, Frok!"

Twitch and Aurora watched intently but saw no movement in Frok's tiny chest. He rested his hand on her shoulder plate. "They're gone, Q."

"But... but she *healed*," Quistix mumbled, shoulders sagging. Hope drained from her body, replaced by soul-crushing agony. Hot tears trailed down her soot-stained cheeks. Her lips quivered. She scooped up Frok's tiny body into her hands and clutched her to her chest. Her body shook and trembled. She let out a soul-wrenching scream that echoed across the courtyard and the ragged cliffs to the gulf beyond.

The elf's tears dripped like warm rain into the dirt between the stones. Around them sprouted thick greenery, weaving itself between stones until fresh, green foliage was climbing the gated palace walls. The courtyard was lush with dangling tendrils of moss and vines, peppered with brightly-colored trumpet flowers. Aurora and Twitch watched with tear-soaked eyes as the stony area before them was transformed into a lush oasis carpeted with blossoming clover. The walls became covered with rambunctious roses and ivy.

Twitch blotted his eyes and knelt beside Quistix. He wrapped an arm around her and pulled her close to him. Quistix pulled away.

The elf's face contorted with anguish, and she muttered with great melancholy, "It should have been me."

Twitch wiped away her fauna-springing tears and pulled Quistix to his chest. "It's not your time."

Aurora stood, stepped toward Quistix, and nuzzled her head into the elf's neck. There they sat in a once-barren, manicured courtyard that had been transformed into a jungle by the power of the mage's tears, mourning the loss of the most innocent and adored member of their chosen family and her beloved.

53

*The Edge of the Glitter Gulf Beach,
Outskirts of Desdemona,
Willowdale*

Quistix stood over two small, heaped mounds of freshly churned dirt in a field just beyond the farm where they'd all gone over the plan just a day ago. It was near the port of Desdemona, overlooking the Glitter Gulf, where the tumultuous seas now glimmered with shallow schools of thousands of bio-luminescent fish. It was a breathtaking sight that many would travel from all ends of Destoria to see once a year. A fascinating spectacle you had to see to believe.

Frok had mentioned she had always wanted to see it but never had the opportunity.

Nor would she.

They thought it a fitting place to lay her brave little body to rest.

"She would have loved this." A heavy weight sagged in Aurora's chest.

Quistix felt like she couldn't breathe. Panicked and anxious, spiraling at the thought of having played a part of any size in the pleom's deaths. Like the losses of Danson and Roland, it was a heavy feeling she knew would never leave her, added to the weight of the baggage she already carried.

Faint, horrific screams of men and women echoed across the tops of the water, carried by the wind in their direction as Quistix pressed the two hand-made grave markers into the ground at the burial site of the tiny lovers who had found each other at the end. Two strange creatures of a kind who fought bravely and lost. She wept for a tiny pink dragonling who wanted to see the world…

And *did*.

Twitch's wavering voice cracked. "*Look.*" He pointed a furry finger toward the ominous, black smoke rising from the spot where the Ruby Palace once stood, scorching the gorgeous blue sky with a toxic cloud of dikeeka. The structure was reduced to a burnt heap of rubble, smoking like a petering campfire. What was once a grandiose castle run by mages with avarice in their hearts was now little more than a quarry of piled stone and charred boards. Damaged relics of a sick time in Destorian history. They glanced out over the war-torn capital in shock. The isle they'd been fighting to save had fallen into a civil war.

History repeated itself, as it so often does. And the irony was not lost on any of them. Quistix stared at the mess they had made. The healed townspeople were devastated. The city of Desdemona was on fire once again.

54

The Dungeon of the Ruby Palace,
Desdemona,
Willowdale

With a talon, Ceosteol drew a circle on the far wall and placed her scrawny, flattened palm in the center. Effortless black magic oozed from her practiced movements. A portion of the stone wall rumbled out like a circular, glassy doorway. She went through it, plunging herself into the abandoned courtyard evacuated by the soldiers, scarred by billowing smoke and layers of soot.

She scooped up Arias' limp corpse, struggling to walk with the dead weight of the akaih nestled in her thin, birdlike wings. She headed back to the doorway from which she'd just come and stole away to the narrow passage within, illuminating the darkness with her glowing green eyes.

Arias' neck lolled unnaturally with the movement, and the portal sealed shut behind her as if nothing had happened.

55

*Courtyard of the Ruby Palace,
Desdemona,
Willowdale*

Several Months Later

The weather had no regard for the occasion as the overcast sky drizzled chilled droplets of fall rain. The day, long in the making, had finally arrived. The exquisite gazebo was delicately draped with flowering ivy. Like a colorful oasis in a desert of stone and grass, the courtyard had been the perfect locale for the spectacle. The fractured building in mid-repair lent a hopeful charm to the event. It was a sign of Destorians rebuilding under new leadership despite the upheaval.

A tune, upbeat and cheerful, was plucked on a lute. It was accompanied by Willowdale's finest voices as they unified in breathy harmony. Guards held a crowd of onlookers at bay before the scorched castle gates. Some booed, others cheered. Destoria's newest royalty had received the anticipated lukewarm welcome from the republic.

Alvanak tugged up the sleeves of his white officiant robes, his parched, leathery skin grateful for the sweet relief of rain.

Arias was dressed in crisp, white wedding attire, moist hair matted to his horns, his wool suit pinging with raindrops. Arias stared at the spot where his body had landed after Exos' ejection. He vaguely remembered the landing as his consciousness faded. More startling was the abrupt awakening hours later. The image of Ceosteol hovering above him with a smile at the edges of her beak tortured him with constant nightmares.

He jerked back to reality with Alvanak's croaky, boisterous holler. "This storm shows no sign of ceasing. May I be so bold as to ask for the covering here, please? I am, after all, holding a priceless, centuries-old book!"

Two guards moved the covering over the ewanian at the podium. The choir members tensed as rain dribbled on them.

Alvanak pulled out a vial of dikeeka from the folds of his robe and held it up toward Arias. "For the nerves?"

Arias shook his head.

"Suit yourself." Alvanak shrugged and crumpled the red wax seal at the top. He struggled with the cork for a moment before he took a nip of the bitter black liquid inside, then smacked his lips. The ewanian licked his rain-spattered eyeball and batted his transparent eyelids to clear his vision.

Vervaine stood patiently inside the fractured archway of the Ruby palace, face done up with light makeup so her scars were still visible. Her hair was neatly styled and adorned with small white flowers. The dress was silk with an intricate lace overlay. The lengthy train took three guards to carry it. Lace sleeves draped down at her sides. As someone who had hidden her face for so long, she had chosen not to veil herself on this day. Her hands gripped a bouquet of white, rambunctious roses on their best behavior. The swell of voices and lute music signaled her. She emerged from the archway into the cold rain.

Arias beamed as he saw his statuesque bride draped in ivory. From a young, homeless orphan to the soon-to-be-King of Destoria, he felt pride bleed through the morose numbness within him.

Vervaine and the three guards walked up the wooden stage and stood in front of the akaih. Arias extended his open palm toward her. She placed her quivering hand in his.

The investigation into the Queen's death had been short. The body was turned to ash in the fire, among dozens of other unpublicized monstrosities. Keeping control of the narrative had been difficult but necessary for Vervaine to take the throne. The collapse of the castle ended the *Bloodied Queen's* reign, staining her short legacy with the powerful stench of bloodshed and greed.

Her death left Destorians divided. Addicted, withdrawing dikeeka users littered the landscape. Thievery and murder were rampant in the cities hit heavier by the sudden loss of supply. Some wanted Vervaine to be hanged as penance for her sister's crimes. Others held tight to tradition. Satisfied with a change of temperament and the continued promises of full coin purses, the newly elected council decided to elect Vervaine while simultaneously introducing greater veto powers.

Alvanak dryly read the 'Orders of Marital Conduct' from a golden, gilded tome that was so heavy his arms shook with fatigue. He rattled off the last of the old-world incomprehensible directives, then perked up as he reached the end. "Do you solemnly devote your lives to the succession of Destoria's sacred principles?"

"I do." Vervaine proudly agreed.

"As do I." Arias agreed.

"Do you solemnly swear to devote yourselves to the progress and security of Destoria and its people under penalty of death by public execution?"

Arias and Vervaine paused, taken off-guard by the newest addition to the official oath. She shivered and bowed to her people, announcing for all to hear. "I do."

Arias grabbed her hand and bowed as well. "As do I."

The crowd began a slow clap, unconvinced but *appreciative* of the display. Alvanak placed a heavy ceremonial crown atop Vervaine's head. The ruby jewels seemed black in the dim light of the rainstorm. Alvanak tried placing the king's crown atop Arias' head. He tried to loop it over the curling horn atop his scalp but sighed, handing it to Arias instead. "You can… uh… figure that out later." He cleared his throat-sac. "Today is not only about your eternal promise to your people, but to each other. Arias, do you promise your love, honor, and devotion to Vervaine Tempest, Queen of Destoria, until you are laid to eternal rest?"

"I do."

Alvanak nodded and turned to Vervaine. "Do *you* promise love, honor, and devotion to Arias Bruis of Asera and hereby the King of Destoria until you are laid to eternal rest?"

"I do."

Alvanak smiled and puffed up his rotund belly with pride. "It is my great honor to be the first to declare you both King and Queen Brius of Destoria. May your hearts stay forever loyal as your love transcends into eternity. You may now kiss the espoused."

Arias grasped the side of Vervaine's neck and rubbed his thumb along her chin. As their lips met the way they had so many times before, something about it felt binding. *Electric.*

As the two pulled away, Alvanak clamped the heavy tome closed. Alarmed by the neon shade, Alvanak whispered into Arias's ear. "Didn't you use to have red eyes?"

Arias replied coldly as if rehearsed. "No, they've always been green."

Alvanak squinted suspiciously, swaying ever-so-slightly from side to side, "I always thought akaih had red eyes."

"My mother wasn't full-blooded akaih." During the past chaotic weeks, his eye color had been a visible problem, yet somehow the least of Arias's worries.

"Oh, right then." Alvanak chuckled and then addressed the group gathered before him. "Shall we head inside for the festivities?"

Arias and Vervaine nodded, turning back toward the castle archway in unison as if through no will of their own. The small crowd roared with cheers and applause, none quite as loud as the old quichyrd in the back, donning a fine gown over her green-tipped black feathers. The old woman flashed her wicked beak and cawed praise, her eyes gleaming below her black veil, just as toxic-green as the newlyweds' eyes. With the undead rulers of Destoria at her full disposal, things were about to get interesting.

ABOUT THE AUTHOR

Heather Wohl coordinates a growing oil field laboratory based in Casper, Wyoming. While her job is straightforward and clinical, she enjoys letting her mind wander into creative outlets. An avid storyteller since childhood, she has always enjoyed spinning fantastical tales. She is a proud supporter of chronic illness support, mental health awareness, and pitbull advocacy, considering the latter to be her furry muses. Her heart and soul are poured into every page of her work, and she looks forward to the opportunity to entertain you.

JOIN THE NEWSLETTER

For updates, discounts, future release announcements by Heather Wohl, bonus material, and more, subscribe to the Rusty Ogre newsletter at: www.rustyogrepublishing.com

Creature Glossary

Aestuo Quichyrd: *(Ah-ee-stoo Kwih-chard)* A hybrid of bird and human with armored feathers, these bird-humans are battle-ready. They have talon-like hands and a beak.

Akiah: *(Ahh-kai-uh)* Often mistaken for demons, a once-forbidden species, the akiah people have been responsible for carrying out various atrocities under the rule of Master Tempest. With human body shape and features, their defining trait is their ram horns and crimson eyes.

Azure shifters: *(Ah-zur Shif-turs)* These underwater creatures have the face and upper torso of a human, and a fish-like tail for legs. Its golden horns glitter below the surface, luring its prey to the water's edge so they can attack. White eyes and scaly skin are another hallmark of the shifter. Unable to speak or be reasoned with, this remains one of the most deadly creatures in Destoria.

Barbarian: Larger than humans, barbarians are known for their large stature and muscular build. Ideal fighters and human-like features make these characters a staple.

Black-Eyed Beings: Creations of Ceosteol who are imbued with her magical essence, having entered unwillingly into a soul-bond with her. These creatures are an extension of her, controlled by her dark magic.

Bramolt Bear: *(Brahm-olt Bear)* Like a polar bear, these massive fur-covered bears fight with their 3-inch long talons and walk upright. Unable to speak the human language, these bears are both lovable and formidable.

Crolt: (Kruhlt) Two-headed giant. Barely able to fit through doorways, these creatures have two functioning heads that work independently of one another. Their shared body is massive and muscular, making these giants a solid protective force. However, their intelligence is one step above that of a symph.

Dwarf: Dwarves are typically three feet tall with red hair. Both men and women of this species grow beards. They are typically ornery in nature.

Eaflic: *(Ee-flick)* Hippo-human hybrid. With gray skin and a massive snout, these creatures are docile until threatened. With rounded ears and a flicking tail, these creatures are undeniably lovable.

Elf: Elves have the features of a human, but typically have a yellow tint to their skin and pointed ears. Adept at magic, elves are typically upper class.

Esteg: *(Ess-teg)* Sentient deer. Estegs are voracious readers and intelligent. They can speak and comprehend spoken and written words. Their unusual horns (which both the male and female of the species grow) are neon green with healing powers. They are often poached for their antlers.

Ewanaian: *(You-way-nee-an)* Frog people. These creatures are a blend of humans and frogs. With slick, green skin and a tacky tongue, these creatures walk and talk like human beings. When startled, their response is to faint and pass gas as a biologically-programmed deterrent.

Frumlan: *(From-lin)* Sentient wolf/bird hybrids. Larger versions of symphs. With a wolf-like face and furry feathers along its body and wings, these creatures can walk, talk and fly with ease.

Goblin: Goblins are people short in stature (averaging about 2.5 feet in height) with large noses. Sly, cunning and often reclusive. Their fondness for gold keeps them from hiding away completely.

Grindylow: *(Grin-dee-low)* They have a long face with rows of muskie-like teeth and eyes similar to an alligator. They have thin human bodies, often pale, with webbed extremities that create swift, fluid movements. They have winding ibex-type head horns and long claws to shred prey. Used to pull ships along on windless days, Grindylows are working creatures that are best never seen.

Half-Elf: Human and elf hybrid with often-blunted ear tips. With lightly yellow-tinged skin, it is truly a flip on a coin as to if they inherit magical abilities from their elvish side.

Human: *(Hue-mon)* With varied skin tones and averaging five feet eight inches in height, humans' greatest gift is their passion and ability to love.

Inelm: *(In-elm)* These woodland creatures live inside of host tree trunks and pry themselves away when danger or disrespect occurs. They are a proud and communicate through a network of roots below ground.

Kleax: *(Clee-ax)* Lion and human hybrids. This creature is known for their long manes, flitting tail and uneven temperament. Fur covers them and long claws make them formidable fighters.

Orc: With skin in various shades of green, orcs are muscle-bound brutes with a reputation for being strong, fearless warriors. They have thick bottom-row incisors that jut out past the lip.

Pleom: *(Plee-ohm)* Miniature dragonlings. Pleoms are small dragons that live for an average of 8 years. Their scaly skin comes in various colors and their tiny claws are adept at lock-picking, making them an ideal companion for thieves. Pleoms typically prefer to spend their time with estegs who can heal them after their clumsy exploits.

Quichyrd: *(Kw-itch-urd)* A generic bird-human hybrid. Unarmored feathers and no proclivity toward magic. These creatures have a varied appearance, but always with a beak and taloned hands.

Raakaby: *(Ray-kah-bee)* Rabbit-bird hybrids bred for meat. These adorable, poisonous creatures produce a hallucinogenic saliva that is used in dikeeka. More than one bite is fatal.

Semdrog: *(Sehm-drog)* Lizard-human hybrid. These lizard people have skin flaps on their heads and scales. Their eyes have slit pupils, but otherwise they have human features.

Symph: *(Simf)* A small wolf/bird hybrid. They are colorful creatures with a wolf-like face and snout equipped with wings and paws. They are small enough to land in your hand and howl instead of chirp.

Tailed Infernals: An abomination created by Ceosteol, these zombified creatures are two wolves crudely stitched together with a snake tail.

Dangerous and decaying, they can be taught and controlled through Ceosteol's soul bond (which she shares with all of her undead atrocities).

Tenebris Quichyrd: *(Ten-ee-bris Kwitch-urd)* Magical Bird-human hybrid. Tenebris Quichyrds are a species of bird people who are gifted in magic. Rare as they are, they are known for causing havoc within the isle, often despised. While not equipped with armored feathers, they wield magic, making them dangerous.

Tundra Goblins: *(Tun-druh Gob-lihns)* These snow-white creatures are violent, seeking warmth in the merciless cold of Evolt. They kill and burrow in their prey. Their fur is highly sought-after and valuable. With long fangs that stick out past their lower lip, these creatures are the perfect combo of cute-and-deadly.

Undead: Reanimated corpses. Undead species of any creature, humans being extra susceptible. A creation from black magic wielders, which is a strictly forbidden magic, only used by nefarious mages.

Landigo: *(Lahn-dig-oh)* Leopard-human hybrid. Equipped with a graceful tale, leopard face, and fur-covered forms, these spotted beings are known for their quick temper.

Wyl: *(Wy-uhl)* Often known for thievery, and superior lovemaking skills. While most wyl's spend their time on *Wyl Isle*, others lie, cheat and steal their way across the rest of Destoria. They come in a variety of colors. Their hallmark face and pointed ears make them easy to spot.

Coming Soon:

The Undead Queen: Book Three of the Illuminator Saga
Releases: Summer of 2024

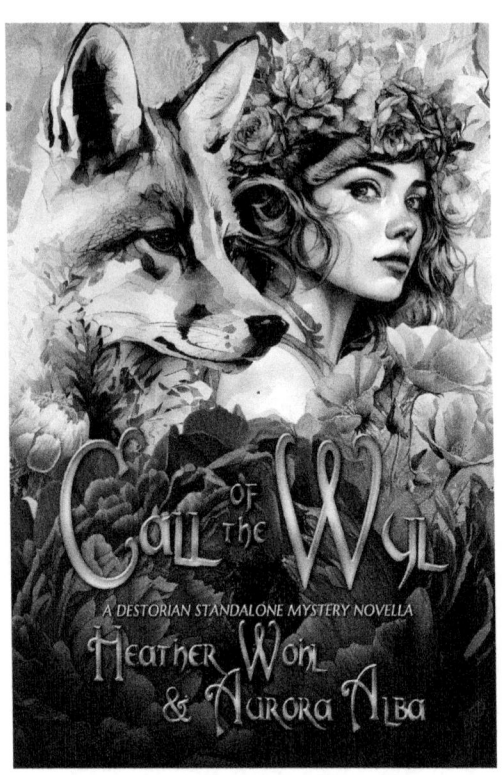

Call of the Wyl
A Destorian Mystery Novella
Available on e-book worldwide.
Also available on audiobook.

How much would it take to send your own brother to the dungeons? With a bounty dangling over his sibling's head, Brutus must bring his elusive brother to justice for the much-needed reward money. On his mysterious pursuit, he's thrust into a violent festival and finds himself enraptured by a beauty, Violet, with rather unusual talents. Brutus must soon make the impossible choice between love, money, and family.

Printed in Great Britain
by Amazon